Streets of New York

Volume One

QBORO BOOKS
WWW.QBOROBOOKS.COM
"We invented the <u>URBANTHOLOGY</u>! Ya' heard me?"

Q-BORO BOOKS
Jamaica, Queens NY 11431
WWW.QBOROBOOKS.COM

(For ordering books, author information and contact information
Please Visit Our Website for the most up to date listings)

Copyright © 2004
by
Mark Anthony, Erick S. Gray, Anthony Whyte

All rights reserved. Without limiting the rights under copyright reserved above. No part of this book may be reproduced, stored in or introduced into a retrieval system, or transmitted, in any form, or by any means (electronic, mechanical, photocopying, recording, or otherwise), without prior written consent from both the author(s), and publisher Q-BORO BOOKS, except brief quotes used in reviews.

ISBN 0-9753066-1-8
First Printing July 2004
Library of Congress Control Number: 2004109257

"Scripture taken from the HOLY BIBLE, NEW INTERNATIONAL VERSION Copyright © 1973, 1978, 1984 International Bible Society. Used by permission of Zondervan Bible Publishers."

This is a work of fiction. It is not meant to depict, portray or represent any particular real persons. All the characters, incidents and dialogues are the products of the author(s) imagination and are not to be construed as real. Any references or similarities to actual events, entities, real people, living or dead, or to real locales are intended to give the novel a sense of reality. Any similarity in other names, characters, entities, places and incidents is entirely coincidental.

Book website: www.qborobooks.com
Cover Photo & Art - Copyright © 2004 by Q-BORO BOOKS all rights reserved

Coming Soon:

Streets of New York

Volume Two

REST IN PEACE
GREGORY GERARD GOFF II
AKA- TRIPPLE G'

January 14, 1980 - February 7, 2004

GONE, BUT NEVER FORGOTTEN.

TO MY FALLEN SOLDIER, THE GOOD DIE YOUNG, BUT YOU WILL NEVER BE FORGOTTEN. YOUR PRESENCE WILL FOREVER LINGER WITHIN OUR DEMEANOR

Author's Note: Anthony Whyte

My turn to burn…
Yeah, yeah, I've got some stories to tell and they're part of my dreams. Don't be fooled because you've heard it all before. It happened à lot during the sixties and seventies when we were babies. How dreams and talent were ripped off by Massa'. Now it's our turn and we do it to each other! When I first got signed, BP sold me on their ideas and that I would be taken care of. Instead they tried to get over on me and then pressure me into giving up more books. Sounds familiar? I'm not about to align myself to anyone who doesn't treat me right, respect me or pay me on time. I'd be a fool! Now that I see they're trying to freeze me…They *think* I can't sign with anyone until they release me so they don't want to even talk to me. I got choices so I choose to take it to the streets. This is my realm and here I'll do battle. First shot is for <u>Streets of New York Volume One</u>. Mark Anthony first approached me regarding doing the Streets…Volume One and I was with it from the jump, so here it goes. And oh, to those that want to keep me down I'll lick another shot and drop <u>Ghetto Girls Too</u> on y'all. It is written and that's the way it's going down. I refuse to sit by idly watching my dreams get raped by Massa'. Everybody talks that talk and what they're going to do but in the end it's all talk. They ain't really 'bout it like that. Talk is cheap …action speaks, ya heard me! One love… Ant Whyte. I've got stories to tell…its only part of my dreams... no it's my reality...

Acknowledgements

It may sound like a cliché, but first and foremost **I gotta thank God** for blessing me, Anthony Whyte and Erick Gray with the talent to write this book and for blessing me with the courage to be an entrepreneur. (God, as I've told you before, even if the subject matter is negative, I got a reason and a plan for that, and I know you know and understand the reason and the plan...)

Sabine, as always, thanks for believing in me and thank you for putting up with me and for not giving up on me. There is NO ONE on this planet with the character, integrity, and loyalty that you have. I'm blessed to have you in my corner 110%.

Lisette Matos, thank you for not holding your tongue when you honestly critiqued and edited our work. And thank you for holding us down with your editing skillz. You smoothed out this whole project. Behind every good writer(s), there is a good editor and that person is definitely you!

Jay Clay – you are the Hype Williams of the book cover designs!!!

All of the Street Vendors in NYC and beyond, y'all are the ones who initially made a market for us to keep writing for. Special thanks to **Sede** on 125th Street & 8th Ave., in Harlem. And another thanks to **Massamba** for holding us down on 164th Street and Jamaica Ave., in Queens.

Winston Chapman, keep writing and keep getting that money!

Nakea Murray I feel like I knew you forever. Thanks for everything.

Natasha Herman, I know you think me and Erick forgot about you but we didn't. Thanks for helping us sell so many books in the Waldenbooks chain.

Shout out to **- Inf and Ray** of Dark Dimension record in Queens....

To **all the haters**...Don't talk about it. Be about it!

To **Q-Boro Books**, its just getting started but we know what our plan is. Stay true to the vision.

To everybody else, we'll see y'all in **VOLUME TWO!**   -Mark-

My World now, is Blacks killing blacks over wealth, fine cars, and priceless diamonds--the platinum they worship -- fucked up seeing my brothers slinging them rocks and killing each other for block after block--fighting for their turf—yo, how ignorant is that, they slay each other over land that they don't even own.

My World now, is racial profiling--cops constantly looking at me like I stay keeping a gun in my hand--like I can't never be that hard-working and educated black man. It's kill or be killed--the NYPD done been declared war on me, but if I shoot back, it's the death penalty for me. They run through my rights, search without human rights, 'cause they don't give a fuck about my life--Police pull me over on a warm summer night, because I look suspicious in the wrong community populated mostly by whites.

My world now...

Wild Side...
by: Erick S. Gray

3:35 am-Queens, N.Y.

"You still coming through? I'm waiting for dat dick," she asked her client. She was up in room 228 of the Executive Motel over on the Conduit waiting for her $100 to show up.

"Yeah, I'm coming through right now, shorty. Give me like twenty minutes, ayyite," her client said, pushing his truck down the Van Wyck with his cell-phone to his ear.

"Ayyite," she said while chewing on some bubble gum and poppin' it over the phone.

"I'm sayin' tho', you charging me full price tonight?" he asked.

"I got to. My daddy is here and my wife n' law and they both sleep in the room. We gotta fuck up in the bathroom."

"Damn, the bathroom, ma...I'm sayin', you charging a niggah full price to fuck in a motel bathroom. Hook a niggah up, luv...you know a niggah, look out...I ain't got dat hundred right now," he tried to explain to her.

"I'm sayin' tho', how much you got?"

"I got like eighty on me. You good on dat?"

She sucked her teeth thinking about it. She had made a little over $1,200 tonight selling pussy and sucking dick. Her Daddy had her out there on the track since nine that night and she'd been on dick since then with her wife n' law. "Ayyite...but you gotta make it quick."

"Ayyite, luv. I'll be there in about ten minutes."

"You familiar wit' Jamaica, Queens? You know where the Executive is at?"

"Yeah, I know where you at."

"Just call me when you get to my floor, okay?"

He hung up and shouted out to his niggahs in the truck wit' him, "This is a stupid bitch! We about to get dat money. She just told me dat her pimp is sleep."

"Word!"

"Yeah. We got this."

The hoe turned off her cell-phone in the bathroom and slowly eased out into the room where her pimp was sprawled out across the bed with his next hoe beside him and they both were in la la land. Her Daddy, a young twenty-one year old niggah who had two of the baddest hoes in Queens was slipping right now. The niggah was sleep when he's suppose to be making that money twenty-four seven. He was supposed to be up on things especially his money and his bitches 'cause that was his bread and butter right now.

Clad scantily in her mini jean skirt and a bra, she pulled out a cigarette from her purse, lit it and sat against the wall near the door and waited for her date and money to arrive. She glanced at the time and saw that it was about to be 4 am.

Outside the motel, a burgundy GMC pulled into the motel parking lot and four men stepped out into the cool night air. They glanced around for a moment and then headed for the motel entrance.

"What room she's in?" one of 'em asked. He was the youngest out of the group, only twenty-one.

"She's in 228."

Volume One　　3

"Her pimp in there wit' her? Cause I ain't going up in there for some chump change. I need dat money."

"Niggah, the bitch's been working all night. I'm telling you, if you see shorti, you know she getting dat money for her pimp....she bad, yo," he explained. "I say about two G's or better."

"Dats what da fuck I'm talking about."

All four men entered the motel where the male clerk paid them no mind. He saw niggahs and bitches in and out of there constantly. It was just normal routine to him. The Executive had a reputation for being the hoe motel where someone can pay up to fifteen, twenty dollar per hour for a room.

They took the stairs being that it was only two flights up and approached 228 cautiously. Guns came out, mostly .45's and 9mm's, two popular handguns in the hood. The one that arranged the date took out his cell and called the bitch.

"Hello," she picked up after the first ring.

"Yeah, it's me, I'm outside your room door," he stated.

"Ayyite."

She went to open the door. They got ready; their gats were cocked back and ready to pop off if necessary. They heard the door being unlocked and when it opened, they saw the bitch's face. All four men rushed in with guns drawn and yoked the hoe up and tossed her to the ground, restraining her but not before she let out a piercing scream.

Hearing his hoe scream out woke up the young pimp and his next hoe by his side. The niggah was wide-eyed when he found himself staring down the barrel of a 9mm Beretta. "What da fuck, yo?" he yelled out.

"Niggah, you know what this is...you fucked up!" one of the men proclaimed glaring down at him.

"Daddy, I'm sorry. I didn't know!" his hoe shouted out still on her hands and knees. "I'm sorry Daddy. I'm sorry."

"Bitch, shut da fuck up because you about to get yours," the pimp yelled out at her. She was in full tears.

They dragged both of 'em off the bed and lay 'em down on the floor. "You got dat money on you?"

"Fuck you!" he chided back.

"What? Niggah, you ain't in no position right now to come out your mouth like dat...don't fuck wit' me, niggah. I'll body your ass right now if you want. Fuckin' test me, niggah!"

"Where da money at?" the next man shouted.

The pimp didn't answer. He glared at his whimpering pathetic hoe across the room and wanted to beat the shit out of her for being so fuckin' careless. Without warning, the youngest one out the bunch rushed over to the pimp and kicked him across his face wit' his size 11 Timberlands. The young pimp bellowed out in pain clutching his jaw as blood started to leak from his wound onto the room carpet.

"Niggah, we ain't fuckin' playin' wit' you.... fuck dat," he shouted aiming his gat at the pimp's head.

"Nah, chill...we just tear this room apart till we find it," the next man uttered. He was mostly the quiet one all night thinking that they didn't need to go that far wit' the violence. "You know dat shit up in here somewhere."

They nodded.

"Take your fuckin' clothes off," they demanded talking to the pimp. "Y'all bitches too. Fuckin' strip...Now, hoes!" one yelled feeling that they were taking too long wit' his demands.

Both bitches started to take their clothes off as if they had much to take off in the first place. The room got searched and torn apart. They knew the money was up in there somewhere. Homeboy didn't have any cash on him and neither did both hoes.

"Got it, yo," one shouted. He had smashed the television against the floor and found it taped behind the TV.

"How much?"

"Hold on, I'm counting it now."

His hand went through twenty and fifty-dollar bills and he counted $2,200. "We on it."

"Ayyite lets be out."

"Nah, nah...not yet, yo," one of 'em said peering down at one of the naked bitches.

"What?"

"Yo, bitch, come over here and suck my dick!" he demanded.

Her eyes were stained wit' tears. "Bitch, you deaf? You heard what da fuck I said. Come over here and suck my dick!" he shouted as he started to unzip his pants and pulled out his dick.

Shorti, doing what she was told and fearing that she might be killed, walked up to him, got down on her knees whimpering still, and slowly but reluctantly placed his 7" dick into her mouth and started to suck him off.

"Ummm...ssshhhh...shit, dats what I'm taking about," he moaned.

"Yo, I ain't down for this shit. I'm out," one of 'em said. He left the room and headed back to the truck.

Within ten minutes, both hoes were getting raped and sodomized in the motel room something serious while their pimp was tied up and placed in the corner doing nothing. Helpless, all he could do was bite on his tongue, scream out, and watch both his hoes fuck and suck for free.

That's the game, baby. Watch out for them stick up niggahs cause they be out there so don't get caught slipping. If you ain't on point, they will come for your bread and butter making theirs the easy way by just taking your shit!

****

Promise woke up to the sound of Jay Z's "Big Pimpin" blasting through his stereo system. It was his alarm indicating that it was time for him to get his ass up and get ready for the long day ahead of him. He tossed and turned for a few moments trying to drown the sound out by placing the pillow over his head but it wasn't working. Jay Z's vocals could still be heard loudly throughout his bedroom. He cursed himself for setting his stereo alarm so damn loud.

"Fuck it!" he mumbled to himself throwing back the covers and rising out of bed. "She gotta get up anyway," he said referring to his company in the next room. He stepped out of bed clad only in his silk red boxers and quickly pressed the power button on the stereo shutting off the loud rap.

He headed to the second bedroom and peered in at her still sound asleep looking so peaceful. He thought to himself if he should give her five more minutes. Maybe he should go downstairs and make himself a quick cup of tea and then come back up and wake her.

'Nah, fuck that, she can't be late again,' he thought while staring at the time. It was soon reaching seven. Promise walked into the bedroom, sat gently down on her bed next to her side, and peacefully looked down at his three-year old daughter, Ashley.

"Ashley, get up," he uttered shaking his daughter gently. "Ashley, it's time to get up. You gotta go to school."

Ashley didn't respond to her father's gentle nudges. She was still sound asleep in la la land. "Ashley, c'mon, we gotta get you ready for school."

Promise threw back the covers off his daughter and smiled when he saw her in her Dora the Explorer pajamas looking so cute with her hair nicely braided up and nestled against her pillow.

He picked his daughter up in his arms still trying to wake her gentle, "C'mon, baby girl...you wanna stay up wit' daddy all night and now you can't get up in the morning. I'm gonna have to start putting you to bed earlier."

Ashley slowly began to open her eyes. "Daddy, I don't wanna go to school," she said.

"Why not?"

"Because I'm tired."

Promise chuckled to himself. "You still going to school. Take a nap later."

"Daddy. I wanna sleep."

"Ayyite, when you get home tonight you're going to bed early, okay baby girl?"

"Daddy."

Promise picked his daughter up in his arms and carried her off to the bathroom to get her washed up for the day. He bathed his daughter at nights so it was easier to get her ready in the mornings. All he had to do was wash her down and have her brush her teeth in the mornings.

"Ashley, brush your teeth properly now. We can't have you going to daycare with your breath stinking, okay."

Ashley stared at her father holding the toothbrush in her hand with the water from the sink running rapidly. They went through this routine every morning so his daughter knew what was up by now. First brush your teeth and wash your face and then come to the kitchen for breakfast.

Promise left her in the bathroom by herself trusting that his daughter wouldn't give him any beef this morning. Yesterday, he went into the kitchen for ten minutes to start up breakfast. When he came back into the bathroom to check on his daughter, he found her fast asleep again on the bathroom floor. He had to laugh at first and then got serious telling his daughter to get up and get ready for daycare.

Promise went into the kitchen to prepare oatmeal for his baby girl. She loved it along with some Fruit Loops and candy too. But he also knew that his daughter needed to eat healthy too. He didn't want his baby girl growing up with weak bones and shit. She was spoiled but not that spoiled.

After he started the oatmeal, he started a fresh kettle for his tea and then returned back to the bathroom to see his daughter still brushing her teeth and playing with the water. It was almost overflowing onto the floor.

"Ashley, what the hell you doing?"

"Brushin' my teeth, Daddy."

"You getting water all over the floor and look at your shirt, damn girl. Why you always gotta make a mess?" he barked stepping into the bathroom, shutting off the water and removing the toothbrush from her hand. "C'mon, I gotta get you dressed."

He carried his daughter back into her bedroom and removed her damp pajamas and tossed them to the floor. Promise shook his head peering down at his daughter as she peered back up at him, smiling. She was a mess.

"I wanna watch cartoons, Daddy. I wanna watch *Wiggles*," Ashley said wanting to watch one of her favorite morning cartoons.

"Later. First we gotta get you dressed for school."
"But I wanna watch *Wiggles*, Daddy."
"Ashley, don't start today, okay."

Ashley started to pout. She folded her arms across her chest not agreeing with her father decision to turn down her favorite cartoon for the morning. Promise started to lotion his daughter down.

"Daddy, can I pleeze watch *Wiggles*? Pleeze, Daddy."

Promise sighed, giving into his daughter's demand. He searched for the remote to her TV, clicked it on, and turned to *Wiggles*. Ashley smiled, "Thank u, Daddy."

"Yeah, okay."

Promise glanced at the time and saw that it was 7:15. He needed to be out the door by at least 7:45 so he was able to reach his 8:30 appointment, which was damn near across town in Brooklyn. He hurried his daughter to get dressed, throwing her in her uniform, a yellow buttoned down shirt, checkered green and yellow skirt, and her cute little shoes. Then he carried his daughter into the kitchen, sat her at the table and placed a small bowl of oatmeal in front of her, telling her to eat.

"Daddy, I want honey and my juice," Ashley asked.

Promise sighed rushing to the fridge and pouring his daughter a cup of red Kool Aid. He then turned on the TV in the kitchen and turned to *Wiggles* keeping his daughter occupied with her breakfast and her favorite kiddy show.

Promise rushed into his bedroom to get himself dressed now. He didn't have time to shower so he washed himself down, brushed his teeth, threw on a little cologne and quickly put on his grayish *Sean John* jeans, a blue *Rocawear* T-shirt, and his beige Timberlands and then scurried back into kitchen to tend to his daughter.

"You finish?" he asked.

"Look Daddy, I spilled my juice."

"Damn it, Ashley," Promise shouted seeing red Kool Aid spilled all across the table and even a little on her uniform. Now he had to clean the mess and probably change her uniform.

"I'm sorry, Daddy."

"Forget it we gotta go."

It was 7:50 and Promise hurried outta his fifth floor apartment in Far Rockaway, Queens. He didn't have time for the elevator so he dashed down the grubby and grungy staircase of his building carrying his daughter in one arm and her book bag in the other. Luckily, he'd parked his X5 close by. He put Ashley in her car seat, dashed around to the driver's side, and quickly peeled off.

"Damn, I'm gonna be late," he hissed to himself.

Promise reached the daycare at 8:15. He didn't even shut his jeep off. He unlocked his doors and ran around to where Ashley sat, unbuckled her and quickly took her out and rang the bell to the daycare.

"Good morning, Mr. Carter," one of the teachers at the center greeted.

"Hey, what's up? I'm in a rush. Bye, Ashley. Here, give me hug and kiss."

Ashley went to her father, giving him quick hug and kisses and began to start her day at daycare while Promise rushed back to his jeep and sped to Brooklyn.

It had been six months since Ashley came to live with her father. Ashley was once staying with her mother, Denise Jenkins, but when she was murdered she came to stay with her father. Promise didn't mind taking his daughter in. He loved his daughter to death and would do anything for her. He wasn't trying to hear his only beloved daughter being turned over to the state, an orphan living from group home to group home, trying to be adopted like he was once. At first, it was hard for him doing what he did but they adjusted and now he couldn't live a day without his daughter.

Hearing about his baby mom's murder fucked him up really bad. Promise couldn't sleep, eat, or do anything else for almost a week or two and even though they weren't together as a couple, they were still cool. They both took good care of their daughter.

Denise was murdered by some punk stick-up kid in front of her building one night in Bushwick. She was coming home from work, getting ready to pick up her daughter from a neighbor when a young niggah dressed in a black hoodie, dark jeans and dirty black Timberlands emerged from out of nowhere startling her and demanding that she give up her purse and her jewelry. He was armed with a .357 and was looking jittery. She gave him her purse easy but was adamant about not giving up her jewelry, especially her necklace which was a gift from her father and had been around her neck since she was six.

The young robber struggled with her for her jewelry snatching off her bracelet and when he went for her necklace, she slapped him. Denise was a tough girl from the block and seeing a gun didn't easily scare her because she was from the rough streets of Brownsville and she had a gun in her face before. And besides, the young niggah that was sticking her up looked to be no older than sixteen and he was looking scared so Denise be damned if some pussy ass, broke hood niggah with a gun was gonna rob her of something so sentimental to her. She didn't even think that the gun was loaded. They fought and Denise was whooping his ass for a minute until the .357 went off exploding a quick round into her chest, causing her to grasp her chest, looking shocked that she'd been shot and then suddenly collapsed to the ground.

The young niggah snatched off her necklace and darted down the block, disappearing into the night leaving Denise dead in front of her building. A neighbor on the first floor heard the gun go off and when she looked out her window and saw Denise lying face down on the concrete, blood escaping from her gun wound, she immediately called the cops.

Promise heard about her death the next day. When he heard she was murdered, he cried in front of his niggahs collapsing to the floor. His main niggah, Squeeze, tried to console him but he couldn't feel his pain.

Within a week, Squeeze and his niggahs set out the Brooklyn streets looking for Denise's killer. They even put word on the streets that there was a $5,000 award for any bitch or niggah willing to come forward and give information on who did it and where they were hiding. They got results the next week. Come to find out that there was this young niggah named Muddy who was known for sticking up mutha-fuckas in a certain hood and that was Bushwick. He had a serious rep out there.

Squeeze and his crew caught up wit' Muddy soon after and they put three shots into his head, one in the eye and two in the back of his head. They even found Denise's necklace on him—stupid mutha-fucka.

Promise hit the Belt Parkway doing 65 in his X5 on his way to Bed Stuy where he was to meet Squeeze, Show, and Pooh, his niggahs from way back when they used to wrestle each other on the playground.

Pooh was the youngest at twenty-one and he had a short temper and could become very loud and violent. He grew up in Brownsville but spent the majority of his youthful years in Bed Stuy. To him, that was more of his home than anywhere else. Pooh was 6'1, a slender niggah rocking a baldy and the only niggah in the hood wit' hazel fuckin' eyes. Bitches used to love that niggah for his eyes. He got a lot of pussy when he was young and he was still fuckin'.

Show, he was a big dude pushing 250. Solid muthafucka and tall too, 6'5 and looking like that niggah from EPMD, Eric Sermon. Shit, Show was always the biggest. When he was twelve, he weighed like 200 pounds. They called him Show because when he used to play high school football, that niggah used to sack the quarterback so fuckin' hard; it was always a show to see. Niggahs and bitches came from all corners of Brooklyn, Manhattan, and even Queens to see Show play some football. It was even more of a thrill to see when the niggah put the quarterback on his ass and sacked the breath out of his opponents on the field. Show even got a scholarship to play for Virginia Tech his senior year but he fucked that up when he got caught dealing drugs on the corner of his block a month before his high school graduation.

Squeeze, now he was the wild and crazy niggah. He was born in Jersey and moved out to Brooklyn when he was ten and had been living out there with his moms ever since. Squeeze was twenty-five and he was the type of niggah that always had to be seen and heard wherever he went. He was that rowdy niggah up in the club or that niggah that was always scheming. But bitches and niggahs gave him love cause he was strictly street wit' that street mentality and that don't give a fuck about life attitude. A niggah fucked wit' Squeeze, a niggah better come correct or don't come at all because Squeeze didn't forget shit. He didn't forgive that easily and that niggah held grudges. And Squeeze, he's not a big dude, 5'9, and 157 pounds with gentle features and a little bit of facial hair. He was a slim niggah wit' short hair but he was a real niggah, gangsta if you wanna call it.

And there was Promise, the fourth. He hooked up wit' Squeeze, Show, and Pooh when he was thirteen after he moved to Brooklyn from Queens. It took him a while to fit in but he eventually did and the four of em been like brothers since then. They mostly hung out over on Fulton and Throop. Promise always had a nonchalant attitude being a cool ass niggah and got lots of respect from niggahs, one for being Squeeze's boy and two, he looked out for many niggahs back in the day when they got into trouble.

Promise put in his Maya CD and cruised into Brooklyn. Under the driver's seat was a loaded silver .32 but it has never been used. He just kept it under his seat for protection. No bodies, no nothing. He had the gun for a year now.

As Promise drove hitting Atlantic Blvd, he started to think about his life and the man he's become. He didn't hold a nine to five like most average folks. He didn't run the streets on a daily basis like his niggah, Squeeze, and them. He didn't fuck around wit' many women like he used to do back in the days. Ever since he got custody of his daughter, the flow of women stopped for him. He spent more time with his daughter now and he loved every minute of it. Promise tried to live a normal life but that was kinda hard when you're raising a child while at the same time you're a Brooklyn stick-up kid. That was how he makes his money robbing niggahs in the hood, pimps, hustlers, drug-dealers. Shit, if they're balling and flashing then they're gonna get got. Squeeze got em in the game like that. He was the niggah that's always plotting and scheming and then he put his niggahs on, promising them that they gonna get that money. Real money, real soon.

But lately Promise been having a change of heart about what he does. He had Ashley to take care of now and he didn't wanna take a chance of losing his daughter by either getting got out there, getting locked up or being killed by robbing one of the wrong niggahs in the streets. He'd been having a change of heart lately wanting out but the money was too good.

Squeeze and the team been doing what they do for years now. They had they ups and downs in the game but on the real, shit paid off for niggahs. They were all pushing nice cars and flossing nice jewelry and clothes. In one month, niggahs might make up to $25,000, maybe $30,000 if shit flowed right for them and that's if they caught a true baller slipping. They might catch that niggah for a few bricks and then they go out to Jersey and hustle them same keys for a wholesale price, hooking niggahs up out there lovely. And sometimes if it came down to it, they might occasionally go out and do some B & E's, hitting up homes in Long Island, Staten Island, and even New Jersey sometimes. Squeeze got his niggahs into all kinds of shit but he was a money niggah, a hustler willing and ready to get that money by any means necessary.

The one good thing about Promise's track record in his life of crime was that he had never killed anyone. Too bad he couldn't speak for the rest of the fellows in his crew especially Squeeze. Promise might have been an accessory to murder, assault, and other shit like that but the niggah never took a life, never pulled the trigger therefore, the niggah can sometimes sleep eazy at nights. Sometimes because being and accomplice still fucked with his conscience.

He promised to meet wit' Squeeze and the rest around 8:30 at Squeeze's uncle's crib. Squeeze's uncle was an ol' skool hustler who'd been in and out of prison since he was fifteen. He stayed in the basement with his girl in a brownstone on Kingston Ave. His girl's family dwelled in the rest of the crib upstairs.

Promise was late pulling up in front of the place at 9:15. He rushed out his vehicle and dashed down the steps, ringing the basement bell. Squeeze's Uncle Junior answered the door in a torn wife-beater and a cigarette dangling from his lips.

"Niggah, you're late," Uncle Junior stated. "You got my nephew waiting for your punk ass. We got work to do, niggah!"

Promises looked at Uncle Junior not even acknowledging his presence and walked right by him. Promise entered the basement apartment and saw his niggahs sitting on an old green couch smoking trees and talking.

"Damn, Promise. What da fuck yo? You got us waiting down here forever," Pooh shouted out.

"Niggah, I had to take my daughter to school," Promise replied.

"Yeah, whatever, my niggah," Squeeze said getting up out of his seat and approaching Promise. He gave him dap and a hug. "I'm glad you came anyway. You know we can't do this shit without you, my niggah."

"I still say you should leave his punk ass out and bring me in wit' y'all. I need to get dis money too, niggah," Junior chimed in swaggering into the room behind Promise, his breath reeking of alcohol.

"Uncle Junior, look at you. It ain't even noon yet and you're halfway drunk. Niggah, you stay your ass home. Niggahs can't be having you fuck our shit up."

Junior plopped down on the couch next to Show. Show glared over at him, never liking the niggah. Uncle Junior was not a well-liked guy in da hood. He was considered a fuck up to most and a drunk to many. It was a wonder how his woman put up wit' him. He wasn't about shit and never would be. It was even a shock that the niggah got a bitch to have under his arms at all. Carina, they say she was too nice of a girl to be wit' a man like Junior. Pretty bitch, too. The niggah must got that magic-stick to keep a woman like her around.

"Niggah, your breath stinks!" Show insulted rising out of his seat and sitting down next to Pooh.

"Fuck y'all niggahs. Y'all mutha-fuckas gonna give me respect in my own damn house," Junior demanded.

"Fuck you, drunk," Show replied. "I wanna see you throw me out."

"Youngblood, don't fuckin' test me. I don't give a fuck how drunk you may think I am or how big your fat ass is. I'll still…"

"Yo, will y'all two just shut da fuck up for now. Damnit, y'all niggahs acting like bitches," Squeeze shouted.

"Call your fuckin' uncle off then, Squeeze," Show said.

"Show, chill out. We got business to take care of today. You wanna get this money today? Huh, niggah?

"Ayyite. Uncle Junior take your ass in the back room so me and my niggahs can talk some business."

"Why, it's my place, niggah! I don't see you paying rent here," Junior exclaimed.

"Niggah, I said take your fuckin' ass into the back room before I come over there and get real on you," Squeeze shouted.

Junior, looking like a punk and getting screamed on by his own flesh and blood nephew, slowly stood up, peered over at everyone and slowly walked off into the bedroom in the back. Everyone waited and watched until he was gone and then they began to focus on business.

"Yo, I got word on them niggahs that be over on Tompkins and Myrtle. They holding serious weight up in them buildings," Squeeze informed his niggahs. "I've been staking the place out regularly."

"So what you saying, Squeeze? You ready to hit em up?" Pooh asked.

"Yeah."

"When?"

"Today."

"Niggah is you crazy!" Promise injected, "We ain't plan for dis shit. We don't know what those niggahs are holding up in there and how many niggahs be up in there. It's too risky, Squeeze."

"Fuck dat. They ain't packin' heat like that. Niggahs up in them buildings are too laidback. They be thinking niggahs can't get at them. They thinking they can't get got, Promise. We gotta let 'em know."

"Fuck it, niggah. I'm down for it," Show said.

"What about you, Pooh? The money's there, no question to it. If we don't get at these niggahs today, no telling when might be our next chance."

"Fuck it. I'm in too," Pooh agreed.

Squeezed looked over at Promise who was still standing, "Promise, we need you, baby. You know we can't do dis shit without you, niggah. We a team. We get dat money together or we don't get dat money at all."

Promise sighed. "Ayyite, yo, I'm in."

"My niggah."

"You got a plan for dis shit, Squeeze, cause I ain't trying to fuck up getting this money," Show said putting the cigarette to his lips and taking a quick drag.

"Of course, niggah. I wouldn't have brought the shit up if I didn't."

"So how we gonna do this?" Pooh asked.

"Like I said, them niggahs up in the Tompkins housing are too laid-back wit' their shit. They slipping, baby. Majority of them niggahs that be up in there running business in them apartments are young niggahs and they pussy. So we ain't got nuthin' to worry about"

"But who's backing them?" Promised asked.

"Some new niggah in da hood from Jersey. Niggah name is Nine or something. But he workin' wit his cousin who's from Flatbush. He got shit stashed in his cousin crib. I say about three or four keys of marijuana and maybe half a key of dat powder. They moving weed in and out of that apartment like crazy. Money coming in, yo. Lots of it. We ain't gotta worry about Nine. It's his cousin we gotta worry about. He got clout but da niggah's outta town till Thursday so we gotta move today. I got this girl that be up in them buildings. She be giving me the rundown when they be moving and where they be moving they shit."

"By why hit em in the day?" Promised asked.

"Because it's too risky during the night. Too many niggahs around and dats when they expect niggahs to come at them, during the night, so they be more alert. But see, we gonna hit em today during the day. They ain't gonna be expecting niggahs like us to be coming through during broad daylight. I've passed there a few times during the day. It be crazy, yo. Them young niggahs be sitting around playing Game Boy, talking to bitches on their cell-phones, and still serving niggahs, and pulling in dat money. They don't be on point like that. Yo, we do it right and we got this money in da bag."

"I feel you, Squeeze," Pooh replied taking a pull from the weed.

Promise glanced at the time and it was 10:00. He had to pick his daughter up from daycare around five. He prayed that this job went right. His daughter needed him after school and he couldn't afford to lose his baby girl over some bullshit.

"This shit better work, Squeeze. I got my little girl to go home to."

"Trust a niggah, Promise. Damn, how many years have we been out here doing this shit, catching niggahs slipping and we didn't fuck up yet? I know what da fuck I'm doing. I ain't no rookie niggah out here trying to get his dick wet in the game. My shit always comes through."

Around noon, all four niggahs hopped into Squeeze's truck, a burgundy GMC, and headed down Bedford Ave toward the Tompkins Houses to pull off their heist. Squeeze drove, Show rode shotgun, and Promise and Pooh occupied the backseat. They all were heavily armed. Promise had a

.380 and Pooh was armed wit' a silver 9mm. Squeeze and Show both had .45s and were ready to use deadly force if it became necessary.

They reached Tompkins in a short time. Everyone knew their job and was planning on putting it in effect. Squeeze stepped outta the truck first. He was parked three blocks away and walked down Tompkins with Show by his side. Their target was on the 8th floor, a two-bedroom apartment. Squeeze knew how these young niggahs operated their business. It was definitely sloppy and he wondered why these niggahs ain't get got for their shit yet.

Squeeze approached one of the young hustler's on the street while he was sitting on a milk crate, talking to some bitch on his phone. He didn't even notice Squeeze coming until he was up on him.

"Yo, son, you got dat trees?" Squeeze asked.

The young hustler looked up and in his presence; Squeeze didn't look like a threat to him or anyone else. Squeeze just looked like some average niggah off the block. Just some niggah wanting to get high but the young niggah didn't know his rep.

"What you want? Dat choc lit'? Dat haze?" the young kid asked. "We got all dat."

"Nah, yo, I'm looking for those ounces. Yo, that niggah Nine sent me through. Told me y'all lil' niggahs can hook a niggah up wit' dat shit."

The young kid stared at Squeeze with quick doubtful eyes. "You know Nine?" he asked.

"Yeah, yo. I came out here from Jersey City."

"Oh word. You from Jersey?"

"Yeah, yo."

"Ayyite. Dat be upstairs then, on the 8th floor, son. Got my niggah, Shawn, handling that business. It's $1,200. You got dat?"

Squeeze reached into his pocket and pulled a wad of hundreds. The young hustler eyes lit up when he saw all that money in Squeeze's hand.

"How many niggahs up there?" Squeeze asked, looking like he was paranoid in front of duke.

"You scared, son? We ain't gonna take your money…you know Nine. Anyway, I only got my niggah Shawn and D up there handling business. They good. Just go and knock on apartment 8D. Give em three slow knocks and they'll let you in."

Squeeze smiled, thinking to himself that this was a dumb niggah; these mutha-fuckas definitely deserved to get got for their shit. First off, the niggah talked too fuckin' much and second, the niggah seemed too trusting and that could be two fatal mistakes.

Show was standing by the corner and Pooh and Promise were already in the building waiting to move. Shit was too easy. They didn't even need a four-man crew to pull it off.

"Good lookin' out, yo," Squeeze thanked, stepping back from da niggah. Squeeze thought to himself that after they were done handling their business upstairs, robbing these clown ass niggahs in the apartment, he was going to come back down and handle son sitting on the milk crate, get him for everything he got. The young hustler went back to chatting with some bitch on his cell-phone.

Squeeze walked into the building lobby where Promise and Pooh were waiting. Show stepped in a few seconds later.

"What I tell y'all niggahs, easy money to get got. C'mon, lets get this shit over wit'. I got pussy to attend to this afternoon," Squeeze proclaimed.

They all walked into the elevator and rode it to the 8th floor. Squeeze and Pooh stepped out first; their guns were concealed in their waistband. They looked for apartment 8D and Squeeze almost had to laugh. He almost felt sorry for these dumb niggahs.

"8D, here we go," Squeeze said.

Promise and Show were standing guard by the elevator. Squeeze didn't want too many niggahs by the door. He didn't want to intimidate da niggahs inside. Squeeze gave the apartment door three slow knocks like money downstairs told him to do. A few seconds later, he heard locks being unlocked and the door opened. A young baby faced niggah answered. He had his shirt off exposing his bird looking chest.

"You Shawn?" Squeeze asked.

"Yeah, Donny sent y'all niggahs up?" he asked.

"Yeah. We lookin' to buy them ounces from y'all."

"Ayyite." Shawn peered at Pooh for a minute. Da lil tall slim niggah invited the two in and shut da door behind them.

Squeeze observed the place quickly. He glanced around the apartment. He was looking for the second guy and seeing how many rooms and other shit like dat. The apartment was sparsely furnished with a run down looking couch, a few chairs and tables set up, no carpeting, the smell of weed lingering in the air. Yeah, Squeeze was definitely in the right apartment.

"Yo, I'm gonna have to search the two of y'all," Shawn said to them.

Squeeze and Pooh let out a slight smirk.

"Whatever, yo," Pooh replied.

Shawn went up to Pooh and started to pat him down but before he could reach around his waist and the feel the gun that Pooh was concealing, Squeeze swiftly pulled out his .45 and quickly put it to Shawn's temple.

"Shut da fuck up and don't move, niggah, before I blow your fuckin' head off." Squeeze warned.

"Yo, chill, chill, chill, yo," Shawn stuttered in a panicky voice. He had his arms raised and Squeeze forced him down on his knees.

"Where your boy at?" Squeeze asked.

"Huh?"

"Niggah, don't play dumb. Where da fuck is your boy?" Squeeze asked again pressing the tip of the .45 harder against Shawn's skull. He didn't want to alert the second man or whoever was in the house.

"I think he's in da bathroom."

Squeezed nodded his head toward Pooh and Pooh quickly went toward the bathroom. The bathroom door was shut and locked indicating that someone was in the bathroom. Pooh stood by the bathroom door waiting for the occupant to come out. They heard the toilet flush and the sink running. A few minutes later the bathroom door opened up and another slender young male stepped out wearing a white T and blue jeans but before he even took three steps, Pooh lunged at duke jerking him by the arm and placing the barrel of the .45 to his skull. The young stranger suddenly began to panic, having a .45 pressed to his head.

"Don't kill me, please...I ain't carrying, yo...believe me," the young stranger said to the two young men.

"Yo, both y'all niggahs get down on your knees," Squeeze ordered.

The two men did as told and rested down on their knees with their fingers locked behind their heads and peered up at Pooh and Squeeze who had them at gunpoint.

"Yo, where da shit at?" Squeeze asked.

The two didn't answer; both men glanced at each other.

"Oh, no one heard me?" Squeeze angrily uttered and to let niggahs know he was serious, Squeeze suddenly started to pistol whip one of the two men striking him multiple times against his face wit' the .45. Shawn bellowed out as his friend did nothing but watch.

"Ayyite, yo, I'm gonna ask again and if I don't hear shit, dats my word. One a y'all niggahs is dying in here today," Squeeze said cocking back his gat. "Where da shit at?"

"It's in the bathroom, the two cabinets under the sink," The second dude answered softly.

"You sure?"

He nodded his head in affirmation.

"Pooh, go get dat."

Pooh scurried into the bathroom while Squeeze kept them at gunpoint. Promise and Show remained outside the apartment keeping watch by the elevator. Promise was wondering what was taking these two niggahs so long. He couldn't help but to glance at his watch every passing minute.

Inside, Pooh came back out with two black bags filled with marijuana and some Coke stacked in keys, dat good shit.

"Bingo," he uttered out to Squeeze. Squeeze smiled.

"You know, y'all some dumb ass niggahs. You know how easy this shit was to get at y'all. But I thank y'all. We need dumb mutha-fuckas like y'all so me and my niggahs can continue to get this easy money," Squeeze said to them.

"What we gonna do wit' them?" Pooh asked.

"Yo, how old are y'all?" Squeeze asked.

"Eighteen," Shawn muttered out with his mouth filled wit' blood, his jaw swollen.

"And you, niggah?"

"Seventeen."

"Listen here. Today, I'm gonna let y'all two niggahs live. But if I hear my name come out y'all mouths about me robbing y'all today, I swear, I'm gonna come back for y'all two and murder y'all. Don't sleep on me niggahs. Don't ever fuckin' sleep on Squeeze, y'all hear?!"

They both nodded.

"Tell dat niggah, Nine, I said what's up."

"But you said don't speak your name," Shawn said.

"Oh, yeah...dats right...you on point now, son...stay dat way from now on. Yo, Pooh, lets be out."

Squeeze and Pooh dashed outta 8D and met up wit' Show and Promise. "We good, niggahs." They all got back into the elevator.

Down in the lobby as all four men exited the elevator, they saw Donny entering the lobby. Squeeze couldn't help but to let out a broad smile, uttering to his niggahs, "Yo, dis shit is too fuckin' easy...I'm about to cum on myself."

They snatched up Donny, beat the shit outta him in the staircase, and snatched off his jewelry, rings, and money. They took his sneakers just for the fun of it.

They arrived back at Junior's a half-hour later and counted up their take. They got $7,000 cash and mad pounds of weed and the Coke to sell off. They came off good. They divided the cash, $1,750 each, and planned to hustle the weed off into the street the next day. Squeeze didn't give a fuck about niggahs retaliating back. He felt that their hearts were too soft for niggahs to come back on some gangsta shit.

Promise took his cut of the money, jumped back into his X5, and headed back out to Queens. Another day, another dollar.

Around five o clock everyday, Promise was at the daycare faithfully to pick up his daughter, Ashley.

"Daddy, daddy!" Ashley shouted out excited about seeing her father every evening when he came by to scoop up his lil' girl. She jumped into his arms and it was routine everyday that he gave his daughter a hug and kiss.

"You miss me?"

Ashley nodded yes.

"Go get your stuff. We gotta go."

She jumped out of her father's arms and went to retrieve her book bag and other belongings.

"Hey, Mr. Carter," Ms. Ways said.

"Hey, how was she today?" he asked.

"She was good but she didn't take her nap today and she didn't eat much of her lunch."

Promise shook his head.

"But she's a good child, very attentive in class, gets along with the other children. She's a sweetheart," Ms. Ways informed Promise.

"That's my little girl."

"Daddy...Daddy, look what I drew n' skool today," Ashley shouted out showing her father a picture of some animals.

"Oh, that's pretty. You ready?"

Ashley nodded her head.

"Okay."

"Bye, Miss Way," Ashley said to her teacher.

"Bye, Ashley. See you tomorrow. You have a nice night, Mr. Carter."

"You too," he replied and then walked out the door with his daughter.

"Daddy, I want McDonalds," Ashley whined to her father.

Promise sighed, shaking his head. "Ayyite, we'll eat McDonalds today."

After their small lunch together, Promise returned home and had his daughter do her homework right away, tracing letters and numbers and coloring a few objects. After, he prepared her dinner, spaghetti and meatballs, one of her favorite meals. They watched a little TV together and she fell asleep in his arms. Promise picked his daughter up in his arms taking her into her bedroom where he began to prepare her for bed. He put her in her pajamas and placed her in bed gently, throwing the covers over her and said a slight prayer.

Soon as he stepped out her bedroom, his cell phone went off.

"Yeah, who this?"

"Squeeze, niggah. You good tonight?"

"Nah, my daughter's sleep."

"Damn. I got a job for us," Squeeze mentioned.

"Damn, niggah...you gonna have to do without me."

"Money in dis, niggah. You can't get one of those bitches in your building to baby-sit?" he asked, sounding a lil' annoyed.

"Yo, I'm out tonight. You got Pooh and Show."

"But you're my right hand. I need you baby."

"I'm sorry Squeeze. I'm out dis one."

"Damn…Ayyite, yo…hit me up tomorrow sometime. One, my niggah."

"One." Promise replied, clicking off, and plopping his behind down on the couch. He was a lil' stressed out. Taking care of his daughter 24/7 and doing what he did out there on the streets was definitely taking a toll on him. He massaged his forehead with his fingertips, squinted his eyes, and thought about shit. He missed his daughter's mother so much. She made shit simple on him when she was still alive but now that she was gone, the burden of weight was passed down on him and it was stressing him the fuck out. He wanted to do him and live a normal life. He wanted to get the fuck away from the street but making that easy money while dealing with Squeeze was tempting, easy, and profitable. And besides, Promise thought, even if he did want to become legit and stay outta the life of crime and get himself a legit job, he had a criminal record and his background was tarnished from his past mistakes. Yet, every night after placing his daughter down to lay, he thought how long would this life of his last? Everything comes to an end and he couldn't risk losing his daughter because she was all he had that was important in the world today. He wanted to see her grow. He wanted to be in his daughter's life constantly. He wanted a way out if there was a way out for him.

Promise ended up falling asleep on the couch dozing off while watching the news.

The next morning they were running on time. He got Ashley up and ready for school early and was at the daycare ten minutes to eight. He got out his Jeep a lil' more cheerful today. He unbuckled his daughter from the car seat and allowed her to run up to the door and knock twice, indicating her small presence.

The yellow school door slowly opened up and Ashley ran inside with Promise following right behind his daughter carrying her book-bag. When he stepped in, he was stunned and completely taken back by a beautiful young female standing in front of him.

"Good morning," she softly announced smiling and peering down at Ashley. She bent over and rested her hands on her knees.

"Hi," Ashley shyly responded with her soft voice, peering back at the beautiful young woman who was a stranger to her.

"And what's your name?" the young lady asked.

"Ashley." She slowly announced her name.

"Hi, Ashley. My name is Audrey."

"Hi, Audrey."

Audrey looked back at Promise, smiled and admired the handsome young man who she assumed to be her father.

"Hello." She politely introduced herself to Promise and extending out her hand.

Promise couldn't help but stare. She was gorgeous. Exquisite. He knew it was impolite to stare at her the way he was staring but he couldn't help it. His eyes were transfixed on her.

"You must be her father?"

"Um...yes...dats my lil' girl."

"She's so cute. Oh, I'm Audrey."

"Hey, how you doing, Audrey. I'm Promise," he said blushing slightly. Blushing around a female was something Promise rarely did.

"Promise," she smiled, "that's a unique name."

"I'm a unique person," he flirted.

She smiled.

Audrey's golden brown complexion and deep brown eyes caught the eyes of many men. She had long silky hair, full luscious lips, and an hourglass figure with breasts so big they looked like balloons in her shirt bout' ready to pop. Promise caught a glimpse of her breasts and smiled. Enticing, Audrey definitely was.

"Um, what happened to Ms. Ways?" Promise asked.

"Oh, she called in sick this morning and today's my first day."

"Oh, well…welcome."

"Thank you. I'm a little nervous," she proclaimed.

"Oh, don't be…you seem cool. I know you'll get along good wit' the children. I see my daughter already likes you."

"You think?"

"I can tell."

Audrey let out a smile. She liked Promise. She thought he was very attractive and seemed cool enough. She gave him respect and liked that he was taking care of his daughter and bringing her into daycare every morning.

One of the other staff in the daycare called out for Audrey's attention. "Oh, um…it was nice meeting you, Promise."

"Same here," he replied. He glanced around for his daughter and called out for her. "Give daddy a hug and kiss before I leave." Ashley ran into her father's arm and gave him a quick hug and kiss on his cheek.

"Bye, baby."

"Bye, Daddy."

Audrey smiled and loved the sight. "Daddy's little girl," she uttered to Promise.

He smiled and causally walked out the door. When he was outside, he shouted out, "Damn, she fine." He smiled so hard that he almost caught lockjaw.

Promise made his way back into Brooklyn to meet up wit' Squeeze and the rest of his niggahs again. During the entire drive, his mind was completely on Audrey. He was wondering if she had a man or worse, was she married? Nah, he didn't peep a wedding ring on her finger. He hoped that shorti was single.

When he got to Bed Stuy, he parked his X5 and went into a nearby McDonalds for a quick hash brown and sausage, egg, and biscuit meal. Half hour later, he met up wit' Squeeze and Show over at Uncle Junior's crib again.

When he stepped in, they were doing nothing but lounging around in the basement and getting high off the marijuana they'd lifted yesterday.

"Where Pooh at?" Promise asked.

Squeeze shrugged his shoulders. "Don't know."

"Damn niggah, why you grinning so hard?" Show asked.

"Niggah musta gotten some pussy," Squeezed answered then took a pull from da weed.

"Nah, I'm in a good mood, dats all."

"Niggah, you got some pussy. Don't front. Dat shit musta been some good pussy. You got dat ill Kool Aid smile on your face."

Promise didn't respond to Squeeze's remark. He was on a natural high. He couldn't get Audrey off his mind. Even tho' they just met, there was something about her that he liked. They kinda cliqued that morning.

"Yo, you wanna hit this?" Squeeze asked passing Promise dat choc lit.

"Nah, I'm good."

"You sure, niggah?"

Promise nodded.

"Pass dat shit, young blood," Uncle Junior intervened reaching for the weed.

Squeeze glared over at his uncle. Even tho' they were family by blood, they didn't get along like that. They be cool at some points but on da real, they kinda hated each other. Uncle Junior despised his nephew because when he saw him, he saw something he shoulda been, could've been. When Squeeze looked over at his uncle, he saw nuthin' but a fuck up in da family. A disgrace to his name. Uncle Junior wasn't shit but a leach living off bitches and begging for dollars. And da niggah like forty-five years old.

"Yo, Uncle Junior you ain't put in for dis here," Squeeze said to him passing him the blunt and doing him a favor, "so don't ask me no more."

"Ayyite, young blood, whatever! We still fam."

"Yeah, whatever, niggah. I gotta go take a piss." Squeeze said rising up and heading into the bathroom. "Yo, Show, hold dat down."

Show nodded.

Promise took a seat opposite from Show, picked up an old Source magazine and flipped through the pages.

"So, what y'all niggahs getting into today?" Promise asked.

Show shrugged his shoulder and uttered, "Don't know...chillin' right now, yo."

Promise glanced around the room real quick. He saw Show getting high and slouching down in the couch. He looked over at Uncle Junior who looked to be in his own little world, still in that same wife-beater, torn jeans, and lips looking as black as ever. All Uncle Junior did was stare at the wall.

Promise was getting tired of the same old shit wit' the same old niggahs doing the same old shit. He shook his head as he looked around the room and thought how many countless hours he spent down in this basement getting high wit' niggahs, scheming wit' Squeeze, counting stolen money and waiting for bitches to come through. Everyday, he'd drop his daughter off and bring his black ass back into Brooklyn knowing dat it was hot for him out here.

As everyone sat in da basement doing nuthin', a loud knock came from the front door getting everyone's attention.

"Yo, Junior, get dat, it's probably Pooh," Show said.

"Man…do I look like your bitch to you," Uncle Junior replied back. "Get da door your fuckin' self."

"What niggah?!"

"Yo, y'all niggahs chill. I'll get da fuckin' door," Promise said. He got up outta his seat and went to answer the door.

"Yo, who is it?"

"Pooh, niggah…open da fuck up, son."

Promise began to unlock the door and Pooh came flying into the crib almost collapsing over Promise.

"Yo, what da fuck!" Promise cursed but when he saw Pooh, his face bloodied, eye swollen, and his gear ripped da fuck up, he became concerned. "What happened to you?"

"Niggahs jumped me, yo."

"What?"

By this time, Squeeze was out da bathroom and when he saw his niggah Pooh looking all fucked up, he shouted, "Pooh, who da fuck did dat to you?"

"Dem niggahs we got at yesterday. They came back yo...caught me alone over on Myrtle."

"What? Yo, don't worry about dat shit, Pooh. We gonna handle dat for you," Squeeze said, getting excited. "Dem pussy niggahs came back at you...how da fuck did they know where you were at?"

"Dat niggah, Nine....he was wit' dem niggahs too."

Squeeze had no more words. He was ready to take action. He got his gat, cocked it back, and Show and Pooh were ready to follow, ready to peel off at these niggahs dat disrespected Pooh. They disrespected da team.

Promise lingered behind. He ain't want any beef.

"Promise, you coming?" Squeeze asked seeing his niggah not making an effort to follow him into his truck and get at these niggahs.

"We don't even know where these niggahs be at," Promise said.

"I know where dey at," Pooh mentioned.

"C'mon niggah...what the fuck you acting pussy for? Dem niggahs jumped Pooh. He family, yo...don't front on us Promise...word, my niggah."

Promise took in a deep breath. He was nervous. He knew how Squeeze and the rest got down when they felt disrespected and truth be told, he didn't want any part of that. His daughter loomed into his mind and he prayed dat shit didn't go down right now. He followed behind Squeeze and the rest, all of 'em piled into Squeeze's GMC and they sped down Throop, all of em packin' heat. Promise sat in the back and Pooh rode shotgun. Pooh's .45 rested on his lap, and Squeeze had da .380, resting next to him.

When they got over by the Tompkins Housing area, they were in luck. Them same lame ass wanna be hustling niggahs were still loitering out in front of the building and Nine was there wit' them this time.

"Fuck dat!" Squeeze shouted. He busted a quick U-turn, sped down the block, and came to a complete stop. He caught everyone's attention. All four came jumping out wit' their guns blazing, firing at their intended targets. Nine and his niggahs took quick cover but they also pulled their guns out and shot back. Multiple gunshots rang out and those that weren't involved tried to take cover wherever they felt safe, ducking behind trees, squatting down next to cars, or running into lobbies. It was early afternoon and niggahs were shooting up the neighborhood like they were in Vietnam.

Promise fired but he wasn't trying to hit anyone. He was just firing just to be firing but he also took cover behind Squeeze's GMC truck and heard bullets whizzing by his ear. His heart pounded rapidly and it felt like it was about to explode out of his chest. He wanted out of this shit and this crazy fuckin' world that he was in.

Squeeze and his niggahs quickly jumped back into the truck when they heard sirens and sped off. Nine and his niggahs also took off. All that shooting done and no one got hit.

"Yo, take me back to my fuckin' car," Promise demanded.

"Niggah, you ayyite?" Show asked.

"Yo, just take me back to my fuckin' car," Promise reiterated.

No one said a word. Squeeze just drove Promise back to his ride and when he got out, they quickly pulled off not uttering a word to Promise.

Promise jumped into his ride and started the ignition. He sat for a while with the Jeep still in park and thanked God that he was okay. Shit coulda got worse out there. He felt like he was about to have an anxiety attack. He ain't never been in a shootout and that to him was a real scary and fucked up situation to be in. He had fired off a gun before but to have niggahs shooting back at you, that was a whole new ballgame to him.

When he got his nerves together, he put his X5 in drive and drove back to Queens, back to his place where he needed to chill out for a minute and be alone.

At five that same afternoon, Promise left to go and pick up his daughter from daycare. He couldn't help but think to himself that he coulda died earlier, coulda caught a stray bullet and died or he coulda gotten himself locked up. And then where would his daughter be? Probably snatched up from him and placed in an orphanage. He started crying while he drove.

He pulled up in front of the daycare and sat for a moment. He dried his tears with the sleeve of his shirt, took in a deep breath and exited his Jeep. He knocked on the door and Audrey answered.

"Hey, you," she kindly greeted looking excited to see him once again. "Ashley, your daddy's here."

Ashley jumped up outta her chair and ran to her daddy shouting, "Daddy," and jumped into his arms.

"Go get your stuff, baby girl," Promise said not looking too enthusiastic.

"You okay?" Audrey asked looking concerned.

"Yeah, I'm alright...just had a rough day," he explained.

"I understand. We all have one. Try not to stress it...tomorrow will be better," she said smiling.

Promise looked into her deep hypnotic brown eyes and returned her smile. He knew her for one day and already she made him feel good. He just wanted to grasp her in his arms and become lost in her bliss. She was all woman and it was a woman like her that he needed in his life. She kinda reminded him of Ashley's mother.

Ashley came over to her father with her things in her arms. He threw on her book bag and began to head for the door.

"Bye, Ashley," Audrey said.

"Bye, Miss Audrey," Ashley said back waving bye.

"Bye, you," she said talking to Promise and smiling at him.

Promise smiled back. "Bye, see you tomorrow morning."

Audrey continued to smile as she watched Promise exit out the door with his daughter. "Cute," she uttered to herself and then went back to attend to the other children left in the room.

A few days passed and Promise contemplated asking Audrey out. Not a date or nothing, he just wanted to chill. He loved her company even though so far it had only been for short periods of times, dropping off and picking his daughter up from daycare. He thought about her constantly.

He tried to chill from hanging out in Brooklyn too much especially wit' his niggahs but when Squeeze would call him up and talk about making that money, he was down for it. He needed to do him and keep bringing in that paper so him and his daughter could live. The other day, they committed a string of B & E's out in Long Island and the other night, they fucked up a pimp over by Pennsylvania Ave and raped his hoe. Promise stood on the sideline watching while Squeeze, Show and Pooh each did they thang wit' the trick running up in her raw too.

For Promise, he felt that shit was getting too hot in Brooklyn and Squeeze was wilding the fuck out. He was becoming out of control. To Squeeze, it wasn't even about the money anymore. It was about the thrill, the love of being out there on the streets and terrorizing, dominating, or causing as much chaos as they could. Squeeze was about making his paper but the niggah was also about maintaining his rep out there on them streets. He was wild, crazy, and fearless and the beef that was escalating between Nine and Squeeze wasn't making the streets in Brooklyn any safer for him.

Thursday evening, Promise ran late when it came time to pick up his daughter. While driving, he glanced at the time on the radio and it was reaching 6:30. He just got caught up wit' the time and the daycare closed at 6:30. If the parent was running late, the staff would drop the child off at a nearby day care and they'd keep the child till eight. But the parent is charged an extra $20 for every night he or she picks the child up after 6:30.

Promise's X5 came to a screeching stop on the sidewalk and he dashed out his Jeep and ran toward the building.

"Shit," he mumbled.

He knocked on the door and felt relieved when Audrey answered.

"There you are. We started to become worried," Audrey said smiling as usual. "Ashley, your daddy's finally here."

"Daddy," Ashley excitedly shouted out. As usual, she came running into her daddy's arms.

"Get your stuff, baby girl."

"You had us worried there for a minute," Audrey said to him.

"I quickly lost track of da time. I'm so sorry."

"That's okay. It's understandable. Things happen."

There was a brief pause as they waited for Ashley. Promise wanted to ask her out but was hesitant. 'Do it, ask her out,' he kept telling himself. He peered at her. She was still close to him but was attending to the three children still in the building waiting to be picked up by their parents. He wasn't shy when it came to the ladies but there was just something about her that made him kinda nervous. Maybe it was the fact that he actually liked her and wanted to spend time with her instead of trying to fuck her.

"Um...Audrey, can I talk to you for a minute?" he asked.

Ashley came up to her father saying, "I'm ready, daddy."

"Give me a minute, sweetheart. Finish watching television."

Audrey came closer to him. The aura that encircled had become embedded into Promise's mind and he couldn't stop thinking about her.

"Dis is kinda hard for me," he admitted.

She raised her eyebrow at him curious as to what he had to say. "What is it?" she asked.

He let out a quick sigh and then just bluntly came out with it. "Are you busy sometime tomorrow night?"

She smiled. "Why, Promise, are you asking me out on a date?"

Volume One   41

"Nah, nah...it ain't nuthin' like dat. I'm just sayin' you seem to be cool peoples and I wouldn't mind chillin' wit' you a little more often. You know, besides seeing you twice a day for my daughter. I mean, if dats ayyite wit' you?"

She let out a slight giggle and stared into his eyes. Audrey was definitely attracted to him, there was no doubt to that. She loved his style and, to be honest, she kinda liked and admired the street in him. She knew he was from the hood from the way he come bopping in there for his daughter wit' his baggy designer jeans, fresh new Timberlands on his feet, freestyle braids in his hair, and the trendy, rich chain around his neck. Audrey thought he was cool and the fact that he loved his daughter so much and took care of her on a daily basis gave him extra points with her.

"You say tomorrow night?" she asked back.

"I know a cool spot for us to chill out at, dance and maybe have a few drinks."

"Oh, that sounds cool. I like that."

"But you sure it's okay, you won't get into trouble for dating a parent, right?"

She laughed. "Nah, I'm sure the folks in here won't have a beef with that. I'm old enough."

Promise smiled. "Ayyite."

"Oh. I forgot."

"What? What happened?" Promised asked becoming suddenly worried. "You don't have a man?"

"No. Tomorrow night, I promised to hang with my home girl. It's her birthday this weekend and we were supposed to do our thing together."

"Oh. Well she can hang. I don't mind."

"Maybe you can bring a friend with you so she won't feel awkward," Audrey suggested.

"She ain't ugly?" he asked.

Audrey chuckled. "Nah, she's cute. I'll vouch for her."

"Ayyite, I'm gonna take your word for it. I got someone in mind that'll probably come along."

"Okay so tomorrow night. It's a date."

"Say around eight."

"That's perfect," she assured.

They both smiled and Promise called for his daughter. He hadn't felt this good and been in this kind of mood in a long time. He felt like jumping up and down and doing cartwheels. The niggah was ecstatic about tomorrow night.

Friday evening came and Promise was ready to roll. He dropped Ashley off with his neighbor, Ms. Watts. She was like family to him, very charming, really nice, and very motherly to Promise and his daughter. She constantly baked and cooked for the two and loved watching Ashley whenever Promise dropped her by. It was a second home to her. Ms. Watts was always dependable when it came down to Ashley.

Promise picked up Squeeze from Brooklyn and jetted out to Long Island to pick up Audrey and her girlfriend. Promise was nervous about Squeeze coming along but he was the only niggah suitable in his mind. Show, that niggah didn't know how to act right when he came around bitches or pussy. Pooh, he was still a young niggah in the mind and the heart. Squeeze, he wasn't perfect, but the niggah was old enough and Promise thought that he'd be the only niggah in the crew acceptable to come along on this date with him. Squeeze wasn't ugly. He was definitely gentle on the eyes with the ladies and he had some manners—some though sometimes he got too rowdy. Promise prayed that he didn't show his true colors tonight in front of Audrey.

Promise prepared for the night and dressed in an unzipped purple velour Sean John sweat suit, his wife-beater showing underneath. He was flossing with his chain and white Air Force Ones on his feet. Squeeze was geared up in denim jeans and jacket to match with fresh new beige and white Timberlands on his feet. He was sporting his blue fitted Yankee baseball cap the gangsta hood way, low over his eyes.

They took exit 21 off of Southern State Parkway and drove into Baldwin, Long Island. Promise followed the direction that Audrey gave to him over the phone. Ten minutes later, they pulled up in front of a sprawling Ranch style home with the manicured lawn out front.

"Nice crib," Squeeze uttered.

Promise picked up his cell phone and dialed Audrey house number from the Jeep.

"Hello?"

"Audrey?"

"Yes."

"It's Promise. We're outside," he informed her.

"Oh. Well, why don't y'all come in? My home girl isn't ready yet."

"Ayyite," he said clicking off.

"What up? What she say?" Squeeze asked.

"She told us to come in."

Promise was 'bout ready to exit his Jeep when Squeeze said to him, "Hold on."

"Why?"

Squeeze lifted his shirt and revealed his .380.

"Why da fuck you bring dat for?" Promise barked.

"Niggah, I don't know these bitches. You never know."

"It ain't dat kind of party, Squeeze," Promise stated. "Leave dat shit in the car. Don't be bringing dat gun into her home."

Squeeze lifted the gun from out his waistband and concealed it under the passenger seat. "You happy, niggah?"

Promise didn't reply. He stepped out and headed toward the front door. Squeeze was just a few steps behind him. They got to the door and before he could ring the front bell, Audrey opened the door smiling.

"Hey you," she uttered, cheesing as she peered at Promise. "Who's your friend?"

"Audrey, dis is Squeeze. Squeeze, dis his Audrey," he introduced.

"Hey...Squeeze huh? Where do y'all come up with these names?" She giggled looking at Squeeze and thought to herself, 'He's cute too.'

"What up, luv," Squeeze spoke.

Promise stared at Audrey and then complimented her, "God, you're beautiful. You look nice."

"Thank you. You're looking mighty fine yourself too and you smell so good. I like that cologne you got on."

"I can't come to your crib stinking and shit. Gotta smell nice always."

Audrey liked that; a niggah like him, looking the way he was looking and smelling the way he was smelling

Audrey had on a denim miniskirt with the shin high boots, a tight white shirt, her breast protruding out something lovely. Before they headed out the door, she would throw on the denim jacket. Her sinuous hair fell gracefully down to her shoulders. Her beautiful presence lit up the room.

"Where's your friend?" Promise asked.

"Oh, she's in the bathroom. She's coming out. Y'all want something to drink, a snack maybe?"

"Nah, I'm good," Promise said.

"What about your friend?"

"Nah, I'm good, luv...thanks anyway."

"Well, y'all chill out and give me a minute. Let me go get my friend. She be taking forever sometimes," Audrey said then walked to her bedroom.

"Damn, niggah...dats you?!" Squeeze asked soon as Audrey was out of their sight.

Promise smiled. "She fine, right."

"You fucked her yet?"

"Niggah...chill...it ain't even like that."

"Whatever, niggah...you know you want dat. All I know is her friend better be just as fine or I'm gonna embarrass the bitch. I tell you Promise, she better not be coming back out here wit' a fuckin' baboon leaching on her back."

"Nah, she told me her friend is cute. She vouched for her."

"Ayyite, niggah...we'll see. I'll be the judge of dat."

They sat and waited in the living room for about ten minutes until Audrey stepped back in the room with her friend following right behind her.

"Everyone, this is Camille," Audrey introduced.

'Damn!' both men thought at the sight of Camille. Audrey was right, she was definitely a cutie. Camille was light-skinned with a slender sexy figure, brown eyes just like her friend, and her breasts a lil' plump, not a handful like Audrey but they were right enough. She had long braids, freshly done, and they went down her back. She was dressed in a white mock neck and pleated skirt, white stilettos that made the structure of her legs definitely stand out, and her sweet lips were glossed out.

Squeeze was unquestionably impressed by her looks and the way she stared back at him. It was on and poppin'. No regrets there for the either of 'em.

They piled into Promise's X5. Audrey rode shotgun and Camille hopped in the back to keep Squeeze company. Promise drove out to Jimmy's Bronx Café, of course out in the Bronx. The four of 'em talked, laughed, and cliqued lovely; everyone was feeling everyone's company.

They pulled up in front of Jimmy's Bronx Cafe around ten thirty. It took Promise ten minutes to find a decent parking spot. Afterwards, the four of em strutted into the place looking like two million dollar couples. Audrey walked close to Promise and Camille was next to Squeeze. The host of the restaurant sat the four near the oversized window overlooking the Deegan Expressway. Being the gentlemen that they seemed to be, both men pulled out the chairs for their ladies.

"Thank you," both ladies uttered simultaneously taking a seat.

"This is nice. I never been here before," Camille said glancing around.

Promise and Squeeze sat opposite of each other. Both men looked like true ballers sitting with their lovely dates for the night.

"So, gentlemen, I'm curious. Why do y'all call y'all selves Squeeze and Promise? I know y'all mammas ain't give y'all them names," Camille inquired.

Promise smiled. "Actually, Promise is my middle name. I care not to enclose my first name at dis time."

"Why, your mamma gave you a geeky name?"

"Nah, I just don't like a whole lot of folks knowing my government like dat," he explained.

"What about you, Squeeze? I mean, what's that about?"

Squeeze let out a slight chuckle. "I'm wit' my niggah, Promise here. Squeeze is what every niggah out there on dem streets know me by and they don't know me by no other name. Dats how I like it and dats how I keep it."

"So, y'all some two gangsta ass niggahs, huh?" Audrey joked.

"Nah, we just keep it real," Squeeze said.

The waiter came over and asked if they were ready to order. Promise told him to give 'em a few more minutes. Everyone looked at their menus and tried to decide what they wanted to order. So far, everything flowed smoothly. Squeeze was behaving himself and the night looked good.

After everyone gave the waiter their orders, the ladies got up to use the restroom. When they were out of sight, Squeeze joked, "Damn, niggah...Audrey gotta pair of balloons stashed under her shirt. You sure you can handle dat by yourself. Her friend Camille is fine tho'. You know a niggah gotta ease up in dat sometime tonight."

"Behave yourself, Squeeze...don't fuck dis shit up for me," Promise said to him.

"Damn niggah, you really like dat bitch?"

"She cool peoples."

"Yeah, whatever. You just trying to get yourself some pussy. I ain't hating niggah. Do you. She a bad ass bitch, tho'."

Promise smiled. "Chill niggah."

"Nah. I'm cool. I ain't gonna fuck your game up tonight. I'm trying to do me, too." Squeeze glanced back at the restroom to see if the ladies were coming out. When he didn't see em; he turned back to Promise and said, "Yo, Promise, let me pull your coat to sumthin'."

"What's up, niggah?"

"I'm working on dis deal right now...major money, yo." Squeeze enlightened quietly.

"What you talking about, Squeeze?"

"Look, you my niggah but this stick-up shit we doing, it ain't kicking it anymore. Shit getting too risky for us out there. I've been thinking...I established this connect, right? He got the product but he ain't got the muscle out there to push his shit for him. He need workers. He need niggahs dat know how to handle the streets. He wanna work wit' us, cut us in. Move his weight out there for him and we get dat percentage."

"What you talking about? What kinda weight do he wanna move?"

"Mostly marijuana and that blow too."

"Damn, Squeeze, dats some serious shit."

"Yeah but check dis out. We move in on dem Tompkins Ave niggahs and take dey shit over. Dem niggahs is weak out there, they can't hold down fort like dat...fuck dat niggah, Nine. We get dat territory poppin and let niggahs know we ain't playin', dat we in charge...and you just watch dat money pour in. I need this long-term money, niggah."

The girls came out the bathroom laughing to themselves and headed back to the table. "What y'all fellows over here talking about?" Audrey asked smiling down at Promise.

"Nuthin', just missing y'all, dats all," Promise said.

"Umm hum, whatever. They probably over here talking about our bodies and shit. You know how niggahs do, Audrey," Camille said. "Like they haven't been looking."

Squeeze laughed. "Hey, I ain't gonna front. Y'all shit is tight. Is it wrong to notice?"

"As long as the two of you are only noticing me and my girl here for the night then we cool," Camille said.

"Luv, we don't even get down like dat," Squeeze mentioned. "Anyway, y'all the two finest ladies in the place. These chickens in here can't fuck wit' y'all."

"I like him," Camille uttered giving him a hug.

"Camille, you're crazy," Audrey chimed in.

The waiter finally arrived with their orders and placed their food gently down in front of them. Everyone started to dine, drink, and continued to have a good time. By one in the morning, the girls had enough to eat and the men wanted to move on. Squeeze suggested that they go to the bar located in the back of the restaurant. The night was still young. Everyone got up and started to move to the bar.

"Yo, y'all go on. I gotta make a quick phone call," Promise said.

"Ayyite...you know where we at," Squeeze replied heading to where the fun was. Camille was under his arm and Audrey was next to his side.

Promise called Ms. Watson's crib to check up on his daughter. The phone rang four times before she picked up.

"Hello? Ms. Watson, its Promise."

"How you doing, sweetie."

"How is she doing? She ain't giving you any trouble?" he asked.

"No, Promise, we had a good time. I put her to bed about two-hours ago. Stop worrying yourself and have a good time. I mothered four children and eight grandchildren."

Promise smiled. "Thanks Ms. Watson. I appreciate this so much."

"You're welcome. Now don't be having that girl of yours waiting too long while you talking to me...enjoy the night."

He hung up and proceeded to the bar where the music was bumping. Squeeze and the girls sat at a small table set up with drinks.

"Sorry about dat. I had to check up on my daughter," he explained.

"Nah, that's cool. We didn't mind," Audrey said smiling at him and definitely feeling his vibe.

They all continued to drink then Camille suggested that they hit the dance floor because one of her songs was playing. She pulled Squeeze up by his arms gesturing that she wanted to dance. He didn't resist. They started to grind against each other, drawing minor attention to themselves. Niggahs mostly gazed at Camille because she had it going on, hiking up her skirt a lil, her legs gleaming in the dim light, teasing niggahs while she gyrated her hips against Squeeze. The both of 'em looked like they were shooting a scene out of Dirty Dancing.

"Your girl crazy," Promise stated.

"Hey, that's her...she be bugging sometimes," Audrey explained.

"Well, she got the right niggah to bug out wit'. He crazy too."

Ashley smiled. "You dance?"

"Me? Nah, sometimes. I ain't a big dancer."

"That's cool."

"Why? You dance?"

"A little. I don't get down like my girl over there but I can hold it down," she said.

"You want another drink?" Promise asked.

Audrey nodded and he ordered her a Long Island Ice tea and for himself a Hennessy and Cranberry. They chatted and the conversation between the two was definitely flowing.

It was going on two in the morning and Promise and Audrey were having a good time until they heard a disturbance near by. Promise looked over and saw Squeeze getting into an altercation with two males.

Promise rushed up outta his chair and ran over to where they were arguing but before he could get there, Squeeze smashed a bottle over one of the guy's head and was cursing and carrying on. A quick fight broke out and Promise who had his boy's back, jumped in and they both got thrown out quickly.

The girls met 'em outside and Audrey, looking shocked but not upset, asked them, "What was that all about?"

"Fuck dem pussy ass niggahs up in there. I'll come back to this mutha-fucka and shoot this shit up…niggahs keep fuckin' wit' me!" Squeeze yelled in front of the girls.

"Chill out, niggah." Promise tried to calm his boy down.

"What happened?" Audrey asked again.

Camille spoke up for Squeeze. "Niggahs in there were hating on us. That's all."

"Niggahs kept bumping into me, yo, while I was dancing wit' shorti then one of dem niggahs had the nerve to step up and stare hard at me like it's my fault," Squeeze proclaimed.

"Yo, fuck dem niggahs…you be ayyite," Promise said.

"So what's next?" Audrey asked.

Promise looked at her surprised that she wasn't telling him to take her ass home. "Oh, y'all still wanna chill."

"Of course," Camille spoke up. "I ain't got a curfew. You got a curfew, Audrey?" she joked.

"No girl. I've been grown for a long time now."

"So, what's up? Where y'all niggahs taking us next?" Camille asked sounding eager and up for some fun.

Promise and Squeeze glanced at each other. "Ayyite, I know a spot where we can chill."

They jumped back into Promise's X5 and headed out to Brooklyn. They ended up parked by the rest area under the Verrazano Bridge enjoying the picturesque and tranquil view for the night. Squeeze and Camille stayed in the car while Audrey and Promise went out for a walk.

"I'm having such a good time with you tonight," Audrey said.

Promise smiled and returned with, "You're cool peoples...I'm having a good time too."

They walked a good ways, staring at the downtown Manhattan skyline and at the Atlantic Ocean, before someone spoke again.

"Can I ask you a question?" Audrey asked.

"Go ahead."

"What happened to Ashley's mother? I mean, if you don't mind me asking."

"Nah, it's cool. I don't mind." Promised paused then he answered her question. "She was killed a few months ago," he somberly explained.

"Oh...I'm so sorry."

"It's cool. I got custody of her now and dats my heart. I can't live a day without her. It was hard at first but I got used to it. We take care of each other."

Audrey smiled.

"What about you? You got any kids?" he asked.

"Me...noooo...I'm not ready for children yet."

"Yeah, don't rush it."

"I don't mind taking care of everyone else's children but having a few of my own right now...it's not happening."

"But you want kids sometime in the future, right?"

"Yeah. I want a little boy first because I feel that they're easier to raise, then whatever come afterwards I'm cool with."

"How many kids do you plan on having?"

"Bout' three. But I don't want three baby daddies...not my style. I plan on getting married first so my husband and I can raise our kids together."

"I like dat. You got standards for yourself."

"You got to. Too many fucked up things going on in the world today for females to be going out and getting themselves pregnant twenty-four seven."

"So let me ask you a question," Promise said.

"Go ahead, shoot away."

"What kinda men are you mostly attracted to? I mean, not just physically but personality as well?" he asked. "Be honest."

"Um..." Audrey murmured smiling. "I like em tall. I like dark-skinned men. I'm not into light-skinned men that much. He's gotta be sweet, charming, and knows how to take care of his responsibilities."

Promise smiled while he listened.

"He also gotta be stable and have a sense of humor. I can't stand boring men. I like to have fun."

"I feel you," Promise uttered.

"And his hygiene gotta be on point. I can't stand a stank niggah."

Promise took a quick sniff under his armpits for good measure and Audrey started laughing. "Nah, you're good. You smell fine. Believe me, you wouldn't have made it this far if I wasn't feeling you like that."

"So, you're feeling me, huh?" Promise smiled.

"A little."

"How little?"

"You got potential. I'll give you that," she stated.

"Ayyite, ayyite…that's cool. I'm feeling you too."

"I know," she replied.

"Look at you, all confident."

"A woman's gotta be in today's world."

"I like dat," Promise said quietly.

"You like what about me?" she inquired.

"That assertiveness in you."

"Look at you, all into the big words," Audrey joked.

"I'm not a stupid niggah," he proclaimed.

"Yeah. I see that too in you."

They continued to walk but stopped when they realized that they both had walked quite a distance away from where he'd parked. They decided to turn around and walk back.

"Jason," Promise unexpectedly said to Audrey.

"Excuse me?"

"My first name is Jason. I thought dat you should know dat."

"Jason, huh. That's not a bad name. It's cute for you but I like Promise better. It's unique."

"Thanks."

"So, Promise, you don't mind if I ask you something else?"

"Nah, go ahead…shoot away."

"What do you do for a living?"

Now that question caught Promise off guard. He wasn't expecting her to ask about his personal income like that, not so soon anyway. He was scared to be honest with her fearing that if he mentioned being a stick-up kid in Brooklyn and a drug-dealer too that it might drive her off.

They stopped walking. "Be honest with me, Promise?" Audrey insisted.

Promise stared into her lovely brown eyes and he couldn't look away. He knew that at this point, it would be hard for him to lie.

"Audrey, on the real," he began to speak, "I do me and doing me is sumthin' that I ain't too thrilled about right now."

"Oh, really?"

"I do what I gotta do to maintain. I'm taking care of my daughter and myself at the same time."

"You're honest at least. I like that."

"I'm sorry."

"About what?"

"About not being truly real wit' you. I'm just scared dat if I told you the whole deal about me, you wouldn't wanna deal wit' me anymore," he explained.

"Listen…I like you and I wanna continue to see you. You're cool," she smiled. "but I'm not trying to be all in your business. You got your daughter to take care of and maintain and what you do with' your boy Squeeze…I understand it's hard out there but think about that little girl in your life."

"Always, Audrey, she comes first. I thought about getting a job but I ain't got the sweetest background. I got priors on my record."

Audrey let out a slight sigh. "Damn, baby."

Hearing Audrey call him baby perked his ears up a little.

"You know what? I refuse to see another black man destroy himself out there especially when he got a beautiful baby girl to take care of. I got family that maybe can help you out with a gig."

"Gig?"

"A job."

"But you don't even know me like that," Promise protested.

"I know that you're a respectful, charming and wonderful man who probably just got caught up with the wrong people doing the wrong thing," she said pulling him gently by his shirt closer to her as she backed against the metal railing that separated them from the sea. Promise didn't resist.

"Why you looking out for me like this?" he quietly asked.

"Because I know a good man in my life when I see one and I can't let you fall especially after meeting Ashley. You need to stand strong." After that was said, their lips got closer until they were entwined and locked against each other, kissing passionately beneath the stars and by the bridge. Promise clutched Audrey in his arms because he didn't want to let her go. He felt that he could hold onto this woman forever. She was such a blessing in his life.

In a way, Promise felt that things were going to become different for him now that he met up with Audrey. He thanked God for bringing this angel into his life. He needed her and his daughter needed her too.

Promise dropped Audrey and Camille off back in Long Island around four that morning. He gave her one more passionate kiss good night and then drove Squeeze back to Brooklyn.

A few weeks passed and Promise and Audrey were spending so much quality time with each other, Ashley included, that they felt like a family. For once, Audrey made Promise forget about his people and his troubles out in Brooklyn. He was having a fun time and he didn't want it to ever end. Summertime was around the corner and they both had so much planned.

Audrey even got her uncle out in Long Island to put Promise on a summer gig selling cars at a used BMW lot. If her uncle liked the way he performed and if he did a good job then he might put Promise on full time. Promise was down for it since he pushed an X5 and BMW's were one of his favorite types of cars.

The chemistry was there. Promise had never met a woman like Audrey who looked out for him the way she did. He was in love with her. Another important thing about this woman was that Ashley loved Audrey, too. She became a motherly figure to his daughter. It even got to the point where he thought about marriage after only knowing her for two short months.

Yet Promise knew that he had to choose between two families. Squeeze he practically grew up with. They'd been like brothers since they were young along with Pooh and Show. Squeeze always looked out for Promise when he needed money in his pocket. He was there. When he had beef, Squeeze was there. Anything Promise needed or any problems he had, Squeeze, Pooh and Show were always there. His niggahs from Brooklyn were like a surrogate family to him over the years.

Streets of New York

But now Promise felt that he had a new family in his life. Audrey and her peeps, they looked out for him in a better way. He got a job for the summer, so that kept his ass out of Brooklyn and mostly out of trouble. Audrey was always there for him and his daughter. When Promise needed someone to talk to, Audrey was there to listen. When he had a problem, she was there especially when it came to his daughter. Audrey became a surrogate mother to Ashley over the weeks.

Who was he more devoted to? Was it his niggahs that he knew for life and had bonded with, or Audrey, the angel that had come into his life so suddenly and became a major reason for his existence? It was either the streets or his *sweet.*

It was late June and Promise was laid up in between Audrey's thick brown skinned thighs, enjoying her womanly bliss. He was stroking his manhood submissively inside her as he grunted and clutched her sheets. He'd been at her place for the entire weekend and Ashley was with Ms. Watson. They needed some alone time.

Audrey lived with her mother but she was never home and besides, she had taken a liking to Promise and his little girl. It was always a pleasure for her to have them both come through.

It had been almost two-weeks since Promise hung with Squeeze and the others. His time was caught up with Audrey. It felt good to get away from the streets, the drama, the problems and headaches of Brooklyn, New York. To him, Long Island was so tranquil and passive. It felt so still out there for him whereas in Brooklyn, there was constant traffic out on the streets and it was so congested with people and problems. The constant gunshots echoed out his apartment window where he used to live in Bed Stuy. But L.I., now this was a place where he would love to raise his daughter and have her grow up. Far Rockaway, Queens wasn't that much of a better place for Ashley to live. It wasn't Brooklyn but it was still the ghetto and they had their ways too.

It was midnight when Promise's cell phone started to ring constantly. He tried to ignore it but something inside him told him to answer it. Audrey told him to put it on vibrate or just turn the phone completely off but he disregarded her suggestion. He answered after the umpteenth ring.

"Niggah, where da fuck you at?" Squeeze shouted his voice sounding guttural. "I've been trying to reach you all night."

"I've been busy," Promise explained. "Why....what's going on?"

"Pooh got shot!" Squeeze bluntly said.

"What?" Promise uttered as he rose out of bed and released himself from Audrey's precious grip. He rested his back against the headboard. Hearing that Pooh got shot suddenly bought him out of the paradise he'd escaped to for the past two-weeks. "When?"

"Yo, we need you out here, Promise."

"Ayyite, I'm on my way....where y'all niggahs at?"

"We at Kings County hospital," Squeeze informed him.

"Ayyite, I'll be there soon." Promise hung up and rushed outta bed. He began searching for his clothes.

"Promise...who was that? What happened?" Audrey asked looking worried.

"I gotta go, Audrey. Sumthin' came up."

"Gooo...I'm coming too."

"Nah, you need to stay here."

"You're going out to Brooklyn, right? For what? Promise what happened?" she asked again jumping out of bed naked. She also searched for her clothing.

"You can't come wit' me, Audrey...it's too dangerous out there for you."

"Promise, why don't you tell me what happened!"

"A friend of mine was shot tonight," he dryly explained as he threw on his Timberlands.

"Ohmygod. Is he all right?"

"I don't know."

Promise was fully dressed and 'bout ready to head out her bedroom when Audrey quickly grabbed him by his arm. She looked gravely worried. "Don't go."

"Audrey, I gotta go. I gotta see what went down."

"There's nothing out there for you anymore, Promise. You need to stop thinking about those friends of yours who are gonna get you killed one day and start thinking about us and your daughter. You start your new job with my uncle next week."

"These are my niggahs, Audrey. They've been looking out for me forever and I gotta see what happened."

"Promise, if you go out there...I know Promise, they gonna get you in some shit."

"Audrey, I can take care of myself. I gotta go see my niggah, Pooh. I gotta see what went down," Promise said.

"I'm coming."

"No!" Promise shouted. "I don't want you out there. It's not your world, not your place. I gotta go on my own. I promise you, Audrey, dat I ain't gonna get into no shit," he assured her as he stared into her eyes.

Audrey's eyes started welling up with tears. She had this woman's intuition that if Promise left her side and went out to Brooklyn, something terrible was going to happen. These past two months, Audrey had never felt so strongly for a man and she didn't want to lose him so abruptly, so soon.

Promise pulled himself away from her grip and left her bedroom. He walked briskly to the front door. Audrey followed behind him and stared helplessly out her living room window as Promise got into his Jeep and drove off hastily. She collapsed on the couch, tears trickling down her face. She thought about Promise and his safety as he made his way to Brooklyn to meet up with friends that she knew from his own words were too dangerous for him to be around.

She whispered a silent prayer and begged God for her man's safe return.

Promise arrived at Kings County Hospital after midnight. He didn't care where he parked. He just jumped outta his X5 and dashed into the emergency room where he was greeted by Squeeze and Show.

"Where he at?" Promise asked.

Show, a somber expression on his face, bowed and shook his head. From that, Promise knew the deal.

"Dat niggah's dead!" Squeeze straightforwardly told him.

Promise shook his head. "Stop playin'...what da fuck happened?" Promise asked staring directly at Squeeze because he knew Squeeze had the answer to Pooh's death.

"Dat niggah, Nine, yo...he gotta go," Squeeze yelled

"What...Nine shot Pooh?"

"Yo, dat niggah gotta go, Promise...he disrespected us, yo...dem niggahs from Tompkins Ave killed Pooh. They gotta get got, yo."

"Squeeze, you know I'm down for whatever," Show chimed in.

"What happened?" Promise asked again.

"Fuck you mean what happened?! Pooh's lying dead and you standing here acting nonchalant like Pooh's death don't mean shit to you," Squeeze shouted. "What da fuck, Promise? Dat bitch from L.I got you soft, huh? You suppose to fuck dat bitch and let her be like I did her friend. We suppose to be family; niggahs knew each other since we were like knee high. Don't dare put a bitch before your niggahs. You should be ready to murder these niggahs right now...ask what da fuck happened later, niggah. Now I wanna know, you down wit me and Show tonight? You gonna be down wit' your niggahs who had your back for life or you gonna diss us for some bitch you don't even know like that?" The intensity in Squeeze's eyes let Promise know that if he wasn't down tonight, there was going to be beef between him and Squeeze later.

Show and Squeeze glared at him waiting for his reply. Promise knew that Squeeze was upset because of Pooh's death and that was why he was trippin' like that.

Promise's conscience ran wild while he rode in the back of Squeeze's truck on the way to Tompkins Ave for retaliation. Promise knew that this day was inevitable. It was the day that he'd have to finally prove himself to the crew and take a life for a life. And now it was for their fallen brother, Pooh. He knew that he had to finally decide between his loyalty to the streets and his niggahs or becoming a family with the girl he loved. Loyalty, he thought, as he gripped the black nine-millimeter in his hand, his heart beating rapidly, palms sweating, mind racing as he peered out the passenger window. He thought about Ashley and Audrey, the two most important people in his life right now. Only they mattered. So, he asked himself, why was he in this truck right now and on his way to commit murder? He had a life now, a future, and yet he was still traveling down a Brooklyn street with Brooklyn niggahs ready to commit a few 187's on this hot June summer night.

The truck was quiet. Everyone was deep in thought. Show drove while Squeeze rode shotgun. Promise's cell phone was ringing insistently. It was Audrey calling but he didn't pick up. He just let the calls go straight to voicemail.

It was one in the morning and hot out being that it was the last week of June. July was right around the corner and the 4th of July was coming. Everyone was still outside their apartments, drinking, socializing, smoking and a few hustlers out still operating business—business as in the drug dealers were still out in the court yards and lobbies treating and feeding their coke and dope addicted fiends through the morning hours. It was 95 degrees and the unfortunate residents in the building without air-condition had decided to keep cool by staying out of their sweltering apartments as they tried to catch a night breeze.

Nine and his cronies were also out, chilling and mingling in front of their place of business and mostly just being on Tompkins and Myrtle in front of their building where their customers could find them easy.

Squeeze's truck slowly turned the corner with its headlights off. They quickly spotted Nine and his peeps. Show put the truck in park and shut off the ignition.

"Fuck dat, we just gonna run up on these niggahs," Squeeze said cocking back his weapon and stepping outta the truck. Show followed and Promise was the last to exit.

Streets of New York

Squeeze just wanted to run up on these niggahs and murder them all. He wasn't trying to give a fuck how many heads were out at one in the morning. As far as he was concerned, he was taking over this area and making it his business. The beef between Nine and Squeeze became personal when they killed Pooh.

They slowly crept up to Nine and his peeps with their guns out and held down to their side. All three men quickly and quietly advanced toward their target but before they could get up on them, the element of surprise was lost when one of Nine's men spotted the attack coming and shouted out, "NINE, LOOK OUT," while drawing his .45 and firing into the night.

Squeeze and Show quickly returned fire. Promise became startled, ducked and then he too started to return fire. His life was now in danger. Rapid gunfire quickly echoed out into the night and folks and residents who were out just trying to enjoy the summer night quickly dashed for cover from the gunshots riddling the projects.

Promise let out multiple rounds at about five to six men firing back at him. He didn't see Squeeze or Show as he darted into the street, bullets whizzing by his ears. In his mind, Promise was on his own. It wasn't about revenge anymore, it was about survival now. They were outgunned and outnumbered.

Police sirens suddenly started to pierce the air. When Promise saw the blue and white cop car rushing up to him, the overhead blue and reds lights blaring repetitively, he panicked and fired at the first oncoming squad car striking the cop in the passenger seat in his chest. The driver got out, saw his partner hit with gunfire and fired back at Promise but Promise had already taken off. It felt like he was running on air he was running so fast. He sprinted through the projects with his gun still in hand, scared to drop his weapon, fearing the cops might find it and trace his fingerprints back to him. But Promise knew that having his gun on him was too risky so when he came to a nearby corner after dashing through the projects, he dropped his gun down a sewer drain and continued to take off running. He heard dozens of police sirens coming in his direction. He tried not to panic and look suspicious but he tried to stay out of the cops' sight knowing that if they saw him sweating, exhausted, and not too far from the crime scene, it was his ass. He would see Central Booking tonight and probably jail for a long, long time if he got caught.

Promise crept his way through the night, trying to be as inconspicuous as possible. Beads of sweat trickled down his face. He couldn't stop shaking. He thought about his daughter and Audrey. He needed to get out of Brooklyn fast. He knew that he had shot a cop and that every detective and uniformed officer were going to be harassing and locking up every young black male they came across.

Promise came across a nearby cabstand but suddenly ducked behind a parked car when a police car came racing by. After the area seemed clear, he quickly darted into the cabstand and told the dispatcher that he needed a cab fast. There was a cab on hand in five minutes. Promise jumped in and told the driver his location. He needed to get back to King's County to get his ride where he'd left it parked and bounce outta Brooklyn and back to Queens or L.I.

It was three in the morning when Audrey heard a loud knock and the constant ringing of the bell at her front door. Luckily she was home alone or her moms would've been very upset at the sudden disturbance at the front door so early in the morning. She wasn't sleep. She couldn't sleep. She's been up since Promise left her bedroom and went racing out to Brooklyn. He's been gone for hours and when she heard the loud knocks at her door, she knew it was him. She prayed it was him but deep inside she knew something wasn't right.

She scurried to the door in her house robe and slippers and relief surged through her when she peeped outside and saw Promise at her door. She quickly opened her door and Promise came flying in looking like shit, sweaty and bleeding.

"Ohmygod…baby, what happened?" Audrey panicked.

Ride or Die Chick...
by: Mark Anthony

3:50 am-Long Island, N.Y.

I had never walked a day in his shoes so I wasn't gonna sit there and start judging the man. Yeah, I was pissed off that he hadn't listened to me and stayed his ass home with me for the night but this definitely wasn't the time for me to start throwing that up in his face. I could tell that Promise was scared as hell and I needed to let him know that I was there for him and that I would be down for him no matter what!

"Promise, just calm down and tell me exactly what happened," I stated while probably coming across like a concerned mother. Promise was still breathing heavy as he picked himself up from off of my living room floor.

"Baby, I can't really tell you more than I already told you... I shot a cop! It was just crazy and things just happened," Promise stated as he began shaking his head.

"Promise, I can help you but if you don't talk to me and tell me everything then I won't know how to help you!"

"Audrey, listen. You already know too much. I mean my world and your world are two completely different worlds. If the cops catch wind that I did this and they come questioning people... I don't wanna put you in a position where you would have to lie for me. You kna'imean? It's like you can't tell nobody more than what you know. So if I don't tell you what I know then...You get the picture?"

I understood where Promise was coming from but he had me all wrong. He was right that we came from two different worlds but he was wrong if he thought that I would just sell him out because he'd made a mistake.

"Promise, look at me! Look at me in my eyes," I instructed as I stood there in my silk robe and slippers trying to persuade Promise to trust me.

Promise tilted his head slightly to the right. He kinda bit his bottom lip and I could see the tension in his face but he listened to what I had said and he fixated his eyes on mine.

"Obviously I don't know what it feels like to shoot a cop. But I can tell you this, my head right now is a whole lot clearer than yours and therefore I'm in a position to think more logically than you. Just trust me, baby! Tell me exactly what happened and you got my word that I'll help you figure this thing out."

I must have broken through the wall that Promise had erected because he sighed real heavy and he looked as if he was prepared to say something but the words just wouldn't come out.

"Promise, trust me. It's not about me and it's not about you. I know how much you love your daughter. I know how real she is to you and I'm not gonna steer you wrong even if it's just for her sake."

Promise gripped the top of his head with the palms of both of his hands and he slowly slid both of his palms down his face and he stopped at his chin. He looked as if he was trying to wipe away the anguish that he was experiencing.

"A'ight, see this is what happened. My man Pooh was the one that got shot."

"Oh my God!" I responded in shock simply because I knew how close Promise was to Pooh, "Is he ok?"

"Nah, the nigga died on the operating table in the Trauma unit!" Promise stated with tears beginning to well up in his eyes. He didn't actually shed a tear as he kept explaining the chain of events to me.

"We knew the cats that shot him. Them punk ass niggas from Bed-Stuy! So you know, I mean, that was our man and all. So we brought it to them niggas. We drove to their spot and we ran up on them niggas and just starting firing! It was crazy 'cause them niggas didn't see us coming until the last minute but when they saw us, their whole crew pulled out burners and started bussin' back at us and the next thing I know is I got separated from Squeeze and Show. I was dodging bullets and I was buggin' 'cause I thought I was gonna get hit but I just kept firing at anybody and everybody 'cause at that point I was just trying to stay alive."

I didn't want to interrupt Promise but I had to butt in and ask a question, "So Promise, please tell me that Squeeze and Show are ok...Are they?"

"I don't know! Word is bond! Like I said, things just jumped off so quick and we got separated and there was shots ringing out from every which way so I really don't know if them niggas is dead or alive...I was gonna call them on their cell but I didn't 'cause if them niggas was hiding out from the cops or whatever I didn't want to get them busted by having their cell phones ringing and giving them away. But anyway, while I was running through the projects trying to stay alive, I started hearing sirens. Five-O was coming up every block. There were marked units and unmarked units driving the wrong way up one-way streets and all of that. I saw a marked unit and it looked like they were coming right for me 'cause dude driving the car was driving like 80 miles an hour up on the sidewalk! So when I saw that, I panicked. I had the toast in my hand and I just fired!"

"At the cops!?" I asked in disbelief.

"Yeah, it was more of a reflex. I didn't wanna get caught with the gun and at the same time I didn't wanna toss it because I needed it just in case I had to buss back at them niggas that was bussin' at me, and especially since I lost my peoples. I was going for dolo. I definitely couldn't just toss the gun."

Promise stopped and I urged him on, "Keep on. So you fired at the cops and then what?"

"I'm almost sure that it was the first shot that hit one of the cops in the chest. It went right through the passenger side windshield and caught the cop on the passenger side like pow! So the cop that was driving, he slams on the brakes and he gets out and he starts firing at me but I stayed low and just hauled my ass deeper into the projects until I found a spot where I could just dip out and walk on one of the side streets like everything was everything. At that point, I think the cops were more worried about the cop that got hit than they were about catching me so that gave me like a minute or two to slip them."

"So did you leave in your car or what? I mean you still was all alone right?"

"Yeah, I was still alone...What I did was I tossed the gun in this sewer and I made it to a cab stand and I hopped in a cab and took the cab back to my car which wasn't even in Bed-Stuy. It was still parked at the hospital, Kings County hospital...So after I got in my whip, I headed straight to your crib... Audrey it was crazy! Word! On the real, I don't know how I didn't get shot! But thank God I made it up outta there."

I took in all that Promise had told me. I had to pinch myself to see if this was all real or not because what he had described to me sounded like something that I would only see in the movies or read about in the newspaper. At the same time, I had to admit that a part of me was attracted to that whole gangsta lifestyle and the story that Promise was telling me was actually turning me on in a *sick* kind of way. I guess it's because that whole gangsta world is so taboo to me being that I never actually lived that street lifestyle or ran with a real thug. Maybe its human nature to be attracted to those things that we can't have, I don't know. I do know that Promise had just survived a wild shoot out and he had the balls enough to shoot a cop. So if he could live through that and survive, then it would be nothing for me to stick by him and help him navigate through these streets as a wanted fugitive on the run. He was street and there was no sense in me trying to make him into something that he was not.

By this time, Promise and I were both sitting on my living room couch. I leaned close to him and I gave him a reassuring hug. Promise seemed as if he didn't want to let me go. His body felt so good and I just kept telling him that everything was gonna be alright. Promise looked at me and then I made the move to kiss him. I wanted the kiss to last longer than it did but I knew that the present time was no time for me to have my tongue down his throat.

"Promise, call Ms. Watts and let her know that I'm coming by to pick up Ashley," I instructed as I stood up from the couch and took off my robe in preparation to get dressed.

"Now?" Promise questioned.

"Yeah, right now!" I demanded as I searched for some shoes to put on.

"But Audrey, it's like four in the morning! I'll get her later at like 12 noon. And if you don't mind, after I pick her up, can me and Ashley just chill with you for one night? I just need one night to figure out what I need to do."

"Promise, you're not listening to me. I need to go get your daughter right now! You sitting there talking about getting her by the afternoon. Are you buggin!?"

See, this is exactly what I had been trying to tell Promise. He had just shot a cop and he wasn't in a position to think straight. His nerves and adrenaline were thinking for him. I, on the other hand, was his only voice of reason so I had to assert myself and let him know exactly what it was that he needed to be doing and why.

"OK Promise, tell me this. The sewer that you tossed the gun in, was it one of those sewers that is packed to the brim with garbage or was it filled with water?"

"Baby, I don't even know. I just tossed it and kept it moving."

"Promise, listen. We gotta assume that the sewer, if it's like most New York City sewers, then it was packed with garbage which means that the cops probably have that gun right now as we speak! They're probably lifting the prints off of the gun and with your priors...Come on, Promise, put it together!"

Promise looked at me and he knew that I was dead on point with what I was saying. I continued on, "Or for all you know, Squeeze and Show could be in the Precinct right now ratting you out! I'm not saying that they're rats but I'm just trying to get you to see the big picture. And baby, the big picture is this; if we turn on the TV news right now and find out that that cop is dead, you best believe that every cop in the city will be hunting you down. Right now, I can guarantee you that they are looking for every possible clue to try and figure out who in the hell shot one of their 'boys'!"

I didn't want Promise to panic but he was beginning to do just that so I had to quickly calm him down.

"Promise, just relax and listen to me! The reason that I have to go get Ashley right now is because the cops are probably on their way to your building as we speak. And if they aren't there now, you better believe that a whole sea of them will be there by day break."

"Yo, you're exactly right!" Promise stated as he began pacing back and forth in his Tims that had gotten scuffed and filthy during the shoot out.

I handed Promise the cordless telephone and demanded that he call Ms. Watts. As I made it upstairs to my room and threw on some clothes, I could hear him explaining to Ms. Watts that "a woman by the name of Audrey" would be coming by to get Ashley in like fifteen or twenty minutes. From the way that Promise was speaking, I could tell that Ms. Watts must have been alarmed but thank God Promise pressed the issue and insisted to Ms. Watts that she prepare Ashley to get picked up right away.

Promise was off the phone by the time I made it back down to the living room. I had thrown on a Sean John sweat suit and some sneakers with no socks.

"So, I'm gonna take my mother's car. What building is Ms. Watts in and what is her apartment number?" I asked Promise.

"Nah, I'm a roll with you," Promise stated.

"Promise, I'm going alone! No one is here at my crib so just chill here and relax until I get back. Everything will be alright."

Promise looked at me but he didn't put up a fight as he said, "A'ight, she lives in the building that is directly across from mine and she lives in apartment 2J."

I grabbed the car keys from off the kitchen table and I gave Promise a kiss on the cheek, "When I get in the car I'll call you on my cell phone. When you here the house phone ring, just pick it up 'cause it'll be me, ok."

Promise nodded his head in agreement and I made my way out the door. As I started up my mother's Jeep Cherokee and pulled off, I remember thinking and asking myself what in the world was I doing? But what I reasoned and told myself is that I was simply helping out a friend. Yeah, he was a friend *with benefits* but I would look out for anybody that I am truly friends with. Really, I would.

I reached forward and I adjusted the car radio so that I could tune into an AM radio station called 1010 WINS.

As I turned up the volume on the radio, the breaking news was about the cop that had been shot in Brooklyn. Yeah, the same cop that Promise had shot. My heart rate increased as I listened and heard the reporter tell how the rookie police officer had died while being rushed to Brookdale Hospital. The reporter also explained that they had one suspect in custody and that the Police department had virtually "locked down" that entire area in Brooklyn in order to comb the area and search for the murder weapon as well as other suspects. Police officers from across the city were doing an apartment by apartment and a floor by floor search of the entire project housing complex in which the officer had been shot.

I immediately began to drive a little faster in order to hurry and get my ass to Far Rockaway to pick up Ashley. As I pressed harder on the accelerator and quickly navigated through the dark and barren early morning New York streets, I dialed my house so that I could speak to Promise. Promise picked up on the first ring.

"Hello."

"Yeah, Promise, its me. You ok?"

"I'm good. I'm just sitting here wondering how the hell did I get caught up in all of this."

"Well baby, listen. Things just got a helluva lot thicker!"

"Why, what's up? Is something wrong with Ashley?" Promise nervously questioned.

"Nah, nothing like that. I just turned on the radio and I found out that the cop that got shot, he died on the way to the hospital."

"Say word!"

"Yeah, they said that he got shot in the collar bone just above his bullet proof vest but the bullet traveled inside his body and hit a major artery."

After I spoke those words, there was dead silence on the other end of the phone.

"Promise? Promise? Promise!"

"Yeah, yeah, I'm here. I'm just thinking. Yo, baby, I gotta get up outta New York for a minute. These streets of New York is gonna be too hot and I ain't trying to get bagged in my own backyard!"

"Baby, listen, first of all, you ain't getting bagged so stop talking that foolishness. Just relax and I'll be back with Ashley in like a half hour. When I get back, we'll talk. I'll figure this thing out."

"OK," Promise said, finally sounding as if he trusted me.

"Oh, did you here from Squeeze or Show?"

"Nah, not yet. Why? What do you think?"

"Well, the news did say that one suspect got arrested and that they were searching that entire area looking for other suspects and looking for the murder weapon."

"God damn! They probably got police dogs, helicopters, and the whole nine yards! I know that they're gonna find that burner. I should never tossed it!"

"But Promise, nobody can connect you to me so you are good for now 'cause they won't be able to find you. Just don't try to call Squeeze or Show. And if your cell phone rings, don't pick it up just let it go to voice mail. OK?"

"Yeah, yeah, no doubt, baby."

"I'm riding witchu and we gonna be ok."

"Audrey, on the real, I love you. Thank you. You looking out for me better than a lawyer would. And that's peace right there!"

****

I had finally made it over to Ms. Watts and picked up Ashley. Ashley was so cute and innocent as she slept. From the time I took her from Ms. Watts and put her in the car, she never woke up the whole time. Even as I drove back to Long Island, she stayed sleep. Ashley was like most kids that could sleep through a plane crash. As peaceful as she looked when she slept, I couldn't help but think how she was so clueless as to the chaos that was surrounding her.

I knew that by me helping Promise, I was basically acting as an accessory to murder but when I thought about Ashley, my heart just melted and went out to her. She had no control over her mother getting killed. And she had no control over who her daddy was, regardless if he was guilty of murdering a cop. I sort of felt this "motherly" need to protect Ashley and I convinced myself that I would literally ride or die with Promise for Ashley's sake.

Well, I made it back to my crib and as I pulled into the driveway, the sun was just about coming up. Promise met me at the front door and he took his sleeping daughter from my arms.

"Take her into my room. She can sleep on my bed. The sun is up and I don't think I'm going back to sleep anytime soon."

Promise did as I instructed and when he returned, we made our way into my kitchen.

"Audrey, why are you looking out for me like this? Be real with me."

As I prepared to cook something to eat for the two of us, I stated, "Promise, two months ago, on that first night that we went out, remember when we were walking near the Verrazano Bridge?"

"Of course I remember that."

"But do you remember what I said to you?"

"Well, we spoke about a couple of different things that night."

"What I'm getting at is this: That night I told you that you got potential. I also said that I can't let you fall and that you need to stand strong...Promise, when I said those things I really meant it! I can't explain it but there is just this connection that I have with you and its real! Aside from my mother, this connection feels realer than any other emotional connection that I have ever had with someone."

Promise smiled an uncomfortable smiled and slowly shook his head.

"What?" I asked as I smiled and began to crack open an egg, "Let me guess. You think that I am just running game on you or something?"

"Nah, you wanna know what I was really smiling about?"

"Yeah, fill me in," I said as I began to scramble the egg that I had just cracked.

"Its just jokes so don't beat me up for saying this but I was just thinking, 'Damn! I must really have a magic-stick!'" After Promise said this, he began laughing.

I stopped beating the egg and a huge smile came across my face, "No you didn't just say that! Oh I see you got jokes!"

I was glad that Promise had chosen to interject some humor into what we were dealing with at that moment.

"I'll give you a pass on that comment," I said with a big smile on my face then I added, "But actually you do have that magic-stick." I began laughing to myself.

When I was done amusing myself, I stated, "Seriously though, it's more than just good sex...Promise, its something much deeper than that."

****

Later that day, Promise and myself had gone to visit my uncle, the one that owns the used BMW car lot. We hadn't gone to talk about getting Promise a job or anything like that but we did go to talk business.

See, I knew that my uncle had a past that was filled with criminal activity. He had been on the straight and narrow for the past nine or ten years but I knew that based on his wild upbringing in Harlem years ago, that he could and would be able to connect with someone like Promise.

So when we got to the used car lot, I introduced Promise to my uncle Brandon and I told him that Promise would no longer need the job but that he did need a big favor. I had decided to just let Promise do the talking and ask for the favor himself so that I wouldn't screw things up.

"So, what's on your mind young blood?" My uncle asked Promise.

"Well, Brandon, I'm a be straight up with you. I got myself into some trouble and I gotta skip town for a minute. I got word that there might be a warrant out for my arrest and it's like this; I drive a flashy X5 that's registered in my name and I'm not trying to get pulled over by the police and in the process get bagged for an outstanding warrant."

"OK, I'm following you so far but what is it that you want me to do for you?"

"I wanna give you the X5 and in return I want you to give Audrey one of your best 325 BMW's. Register it in her name and all of that. But the thing is I don't want you to resell the X5. I want you to chop it and sell the parts. I know that'll be a lot of work for you but in the end, you'll get more money from chopping the X5 than any of the 325's on this lot are worth!"

My uncle Brandon placed a toothpick in the corner of his mouth and he twirled it a bit. He was deep in thought and he scoped Promise up and down as if he was trying to look right into his soul. My uncle also looked at me before finally speaking up.

"No dice. Look young blood, you see this young lady right here? She is like a daughter to me. She ain't never been in no trouble before and I'm not trying to see anything happen to her. I definitely ain't trying to see her catch a charge on the count of you. I understand your situation but I'm not co-signing on that. Like I said, no dice."

I wanted to jump in and speak up for myself but Promise spoke up before I could form my words.

"OK, no problem. I respect that and I understand where you're coming from," Promise said as he reached out his hand and gave my uncle a pound.

"Wait a minute. Uncle Brandon. Look at me."

My uncle looked at me and waited to hear what I had to say. As workers and other customers milled around the used car lot, I spoke to my uncle on Promise's behalf.

"Uncle Brandon, for as long as you've known me I have never once asked you for anything. Yet it was you, when my mother died, who told me that if I ever needed anything to not hesitate to ask you for it. You told me that when I was thirteen years old. And now that I'm twenty-two, I wanna believe that your offer to be there for me is still on the table. Yeah, I know you don't know Promise and I understand that but you know me. Please, just trust me on this! Please... Uncle Brandon, you know if there was anything like somebody forcing my hand to do something that I didn't wanna do that I would reach out to you and have you *handle* it for me. So what I'm saying is that this idea to chop the X5 is *our* idea. I'm co-signing on it and I'm asking you to co-sign on it for us."

My uncle took two steps away from us and he glanced over to look at something that was happening on the lot. He then turned back to us and he paused before he spoke.

"Young blood, leave the car here with me. I'm a take care of it. But let me explain something to you and trust these words 'cause I say what I mean and I mean what I say! I've done more years in the joint than you've been alive. So it's nothing for me to go back to the joint. You can check my stats and find out if it ain't true that I've killed niggas with these two hands for showing me the smallest bit of disrespect. And I say that to say this; if you slip up and get my niece caught out there or if you disrespect her in the slightest way. God help yo ass. I don't know what you got going down and I don't wanna know but I do know that if I see any police coming around here sniffing and checking around then that also will be yo ass. You see how calm I'm talking? That's because what I'm saying is not a threat, its straight up the truth. Ain't nobody more OG than me and I won't hesitate to bring to your young ass so you better know what the hell you doing, young blood."

So everything worked out good with my uncle. He took the X5 and he gave me a late model black 325. He took care of getting the registration, the plates, and the inspection. With his connections at the DMV and with insurance agents, he was able to get it done within a matter of hours so that helped out a whole lot 'cause things had began to heat up something crazy!

****

Promise's cell phone had been ringing off the hook. The majority of the time, Promise recognized the numbers on the caller ID as being either Squeeze or Show. Promise put his phone on speaker mode and he played one of the messages that Squeeze had left and I listened in.

"Yo kid, where you at, nigga!? I'm making sure that you a'ight. I hope you ain't get bagged. Call me back nigga! It's Squeeze. Hey, yo, Nine and them stupid niggas shot a cop when we ran up on them that night. Them niggas is so stupid! One!"

After Promise was done listening to the message, I immediately told him to not even think about calling back Squeeze or Show. How did Squeeze know that Nine and his crew had shot the cop? That probably was game. The cops were probably making him leave a message like that. I wasn't trusting anybody. In fact, I had Promise call Nextel's customer service and totally disconnect the service to his phone. I felt that for the time being that he had to totally distance himself from anything that could help the cops catch him. The last thing that he needed was a damn cell phone tripping him up.

But as I mentioned earlier, things had began to heat up something crazy. Apparently, the cops had found the murder weapon that Promise used because it was all over the news that the police were running ballistics tests on a gun that they found and were trying to determine if it was the murder weapon used to kill the officer. The police were also saying how they were close to releasing a photo of the lead suspect believed to be the shooter in the murder of the cop.

We really felt the heat when Ms. Watts had called Promise just prior to him disconnecting his cell phone with Nextel. As he spoke to Ms. Watts, I stood nearby and from the gist of the conversation, I could tell exactly what the hell was going on. I immediately became so pissed off with myself and I couldn't believe that I had slipped up the way I had. I wanted to kick myself for being so stupid!

When Promise got off the phone, he immediately began telling me what Ms. Watts had said, "Yo, the cops were just at Ms. Watts' crib asking her if she'd seen me!"

"Promise, I could tell that from the flow of the conversation. So what did she tell them?"

"Well, first of all, she was all freaked out because she said that they had a search warrant and that they came in like gang busters tearing the place apart looking for my ass. She said that they told her that I had killed a cop and that if she knew anything about where I was at that she had to tell them or she could risk getting locked up!"

I shook my head and just thought about what move to make. I could tell that Promise was nervous as hell. I also knew that I had slipped up by having Promise tell Ms. Watts my real name and exactly who I was. I was so stupid! All I had to do was tell him to tell Ms. Watts some fake name and we would've been a'ight. The cops had no way of connecting me to Promise. That was until they had spoken to Ms. Watts!

"So, did she say that she knew where you were at or anything like that?"

"Nah, she don't know where I'm at but..."

I interrupted Promise and finished off his words, "But she told the cops that a woman named *'Audrey'* came by in the wee hours of the morning and picked up his daughter."

Promise paced the floor and I could see the anguish on his face. "Promise, I'm sorry. I should have told you to give Ms. Watts a fake name for me when I went to pick up Ashley."

"Audrey, what the hell are you apologizing for!?" Promise shouted, "If it wasn't for you insisting that Ashley get picked up right away then who knows what would have happened. I mean, I could have got knocked going to pick her up or something, I don't know."

Finally, Promise began to take charge and assert himself. "Yo, we were one step ahead of the cops by picking up Ashley when we did and we gotta stay one step ahead of them now. I mean, I know that after they left Ms. Watts that they probably headed straight to the daycare center. And how is it gonna look when they get to the daycare center and find out that Ashley is absent on the same day that her teacher named *Audrey* called in sick?"

"But, Promise, that ain't nothing 'cause I was only a temporary worker there. It's not like I was a full time staff member or something like that. If I never go back to that job, it won't mean nothing."

"Yeah but that's really neither here nor there. The thing that I am getting at is that the cops are gonna follow any and every lead. For all we know, they could be on their way to your crib right now! Baby, we gotta bounce! Go upstairs and get Ashley. I know what we gonna do but I need you to ride with me."

"Promise, you know I'm riding with you!"

Without hesitation, I grabbed Ashley and the three of us quickly jumped in the 325 and made our way onto the Southern State Parkway. As we drove, I was thinking that we might be heading to a hotel or something. I didn't know if Promise had any money on him but it was ok because I had my credit card and about $300 in my bag so I figured that the cash alone would be enough to cover the hotel expenses for a day or two. If we needed more money then I would just have to use my plastic.

"Audrey, get off at the Linden Blvd exit in Elmont," Promise instructed.

"Exit 13?" I curiously asked while thinking to myself that there weren't any hotels or motels in that area.

"Yeah, I gotta make a stop at the bank," Promise nonchalantly replied.

"Nah, I got money. I got like $300 on me. I don't think you should use no ATM machines or anything like that. You know with the cameras and all, you don't want the cops tracing back the transactions."

"I'm good. Don't worry about it. Just get off at Linden Blvd and go to ECSB."

I didn't like Promise's idea of stopping at a bank but I did as I was instructed. I exited off the parkway and pulled into the first sparking space that I saw which was about a half block away from the East Coast Savings Bank. Promise got out and he told me that he would be right back.

As I watched him walk his sexy ass into the bank, I couldn't help but think about how nice the weather was. But unfortunately, when you're on the run from the police there ain't much time to enjoy the good weather. As I sat with the engine idling, Ashley asked me if I could turn up the stereo so that she could hear her favorite Beyonce song. While turning up the music, I couldn't help but melt when I looked at her sitting in her booster seat as she began moving to the rhythm of *Dangerously In Love*. After about ten minutes, maybe less than that, Promise came back to the car in a rushed fashion.

"Hurry up and pull off baby!" he instructed sounding kind of nervous.

"Why? What happened?"

"Audrey, just drive! Get on the Cross Island Parkway and head towards the Verrazano Bridge! Hurry up! Go!"

I did as I was told but I couldn't help but wonder if Promise had seen a cop or what. I didn't know what to think. Promise reclined his seat all the way back. I could see his chest rapidly rising and falling as if he were hyperventilating.

"Promise, you ok?"

"Yeah, yeah, I'm good. I'm good," Promise said as he exhaled very deeply.

As soon as he saw that we were back on the Parkway, he let out a sinister smile as he handed me a bulging white envelope.

"What's that?"

"I think its like five grand. I just got them niggas!"

"You just got them niggas? What are you talking about?"

"The bank, I just robbed them."

"Promise, you just robbed the bank!?" I asked in a bit of disbelief, shock, and disgust.

"Yes, the bank!"

"Promise, no you did not just rob that damn bank! What the hell!?"

Promise took the envelope from me and he began to count the money right in front of me without any regards for his daughter who was watching and listening to everything that was going on.

"Promise, are you serious?"

"Yes, baby! I'm dead ass! This is me! I'm a stick up kid. This is what I do and this is what I know. We gotta skip town and we gotta get this money so we can live. I ain't never had a ATM card or a bank account in my entire life! This is how I do my banking!"

Promise paused and then he added, "Look! Robbing a bank, that ain't what I wanna be doing, especially with my daughter in the car wit' me! But I'm just doing what I gotta do! I mean every cop in the city is looking for me, and baby I ain't got too many options right now!"

"But, Promise, I told you I got like $300 on me and I got my credit card with me."

"Audrey, listen, I want us to make it to Virginia, the Hampton Roads area. And when we get there, we're gonna need money! I got a daughter, I got you, I got the cops looking for me, and its not like I can just up and get a job at Home Depot or something!"

I didn't respond to Promise. I just looked straight ahead and I kept my eyes on the road. Finally, I had been slapped with a dose of reality as I listened to the music coming out of the speakers. The reality was that I was rolling with a straight up thug! I couldn't fathom how he could shoot a cop, kill the cop at that, and then in a relatively short time thereafter, just walk into a bank as calm as hell and rob the joint! OK, the cop killing thing, I could explain that away and say that it was a reflex thing where he'd just gotten caught up in the heat of the moment. But the bank robbing thing? I couldn't get it.

Promise explained to me how he just went to a counter inside the bank and acted like he was filling out a withdrawal slip but in actuality he was really writing a note instructing the teller that he had a gun and that he wanted her to quickly take all of the money in her draw and put it inside an envelope. He then got on the line for business banking customers since those tellers held the most money in their drawers and he passed the teller the note. In a flash, she handed him the money and he bounced.

After listening to him detail his criminal act of bank robbery, I watched Promise gleefully count his loot and when he was done counting, he spoke up, "$5600, baby! That's not bad for five minutes worth of work, right?"

In disbelief and with a somewhat hidden disgust for Promise's flagrant attitude, I reached forward and I changed the radio station. Ironically, 50 Cent's hit song <u>What Up Gangsta </u>was on. I looked at Promise and I nodded at him to pretend as if I was in agreement with his suggestion that the $5600 was in deed *good pay* for five minutes of *work*.

"Yo, yo, yo turn that up! Turn that up! Yeah! I love this nigga, Fifty!"

I turned up the music but apparently I hadn't turned it up loud enough. Promise reached the volume button with his index finger and he turned the music as loud as it would go. As I drove and navigated through a developing parkway traffic jam, I listened as Promise shouted the hook to the song as loud as he could, "What up blood, what up cuz, what up blood, what up *gaaangsterrr*!"

At that moment, it was confirmed that Promise and myself had to have been *wired* different at birth or something! Finally, for my eardrum's sake, the song ended and Promise lowered the volume. With the radio now at a decent decibel, Promise continued to amaze me by coming across so detached from the circumstances that we were in.

Promise turned around and looked at Ashley and showed her all of the money that *Daddy had made.* Then he asked, "Do you wanna go to McDonald's, baby girl?"

Of course, Ashley agreed. What kid would turn down McDonald's? So Promise ordered me to get off the parkway and to plot a course to the nearest McDonald's so that he could purchase a Happy Meal for his baby girl.

****

I had successfully driven for about three or four hours. We were traveling south on I-95 and I am almost sure that we were in the state of Maryland when my mother's cell phone number showed up on the caller ID of my cell phone. I turned down the music so that I would be able to hear what my mother had to say.

"Hey Mom," I said as tried to sound as calm and normal as ever.

"Audrey, where the hell are you at!?" My mother uncharacteristically screamed into my ear almost rupturing my eardrum.

Before I could answer, my mother continued on, "I knew that nigga was no good! I knew it! With a name like 'Promise,' I should have never gone against my instincts. That boy ain't nothing but a damn thug! And what kind of name is that anyway? He ain't nothing but a broken Promise!"

I looked at Promise and I stretched open my right hand so that my four outstretched fingers could sort of make an opening and closing motion with my thumb. I was trying to indicate to Promise that the person on the other end of the phone was yapping away.

"Who is that?" Promise silently mouthed to me.

"My mother," I silently mouthed back.

Promise nodded his head and reclined back in his seat.

"Mom...mom..."

My mother would not let me get in a word without her stepping on my words.

"Audrey, are you with that boy? Answer me, Audrey!"

"Mom, I will answer you but every time that I try to speak you talk right over me. So are you gonna let me speak?"

"Audrey, don't try to get all smart and sassy with me! Not when I come home to a block full of cops and police, and the damn news media saying that my home is suspected of possibly housing a fugitive! Do you know how embarrassing that is? Now, tell me, how do I explain that?"

"Hello...Hello...Mom? Can you hear me? Hello? You're breaking up...Let me call you back."

Although I was faking and acting like the phone had static, I immediately hung up the phone 'cause I just didn't wanna hear what else that my mother had to say. I knew that eventually I would have to hear her mouth but I felt that she needed at least a day or two to marinate and cool down.

"The cops are at my moms crib," I informed Promise. I made sure not to tell him what my mother had said about him.

"You see that? I'm glad that we left when we did," Promise calmly stated, "The cops, man I tell you," Promise continued on while sitting upright and shaking his head, "They know how to hunt a nigga down when its one of *them* that gets taken out but let it have been a *black nigger* from the ghetto who got killed. You think they would care and be following leads the way they doing with me? *Hellll no*."

My cell phone began to ring again and I quickly turned off the phone. At that point, all kinds of emotions and thoughts were beginning to fill my head as to just what in the hell was I doing. Promise must have sensed the doubt that was starting to get the best of me and he chimed in and took the conversation in the only possible direction that could have taken my mind off of saying "to hell with this whole running from the police ordeal!"

"Audrey, something that I don't understand about you is this; When we were talking to your uncle about chopping up the X5 and getting this car that we're in, you mentioned to him something about when your moms died when you were thirteen... But a minute ago, you were just talking to your moms on the phone. So, how could that be if your *moms* is dead?"

Promise looked at me intently and waited for my answer. Little did he know but he was tapping into one of the major motivators that allowed me to ride with him and his daughter on the ordeal that he was going though.

"Well, I rarely ever talk about this with anyone but when I was turning twelve years old, my mother was diagnosed with cancer. And it was always just me and my moms for as long as I could remember. I've seen pictures of my pops but I don't remember him. I never got a chance to meet him and talk with him before he died when I was young. So, it was always just me and my moms and when she got sick, she and I couldn't do the things that we used to do. Emotionally, she just couldn't be there for me anymore. That whole year that she battled cancer, well, that was the toughest year of my life because I watched my mother live in pain and basically die a slow death. Before I knew it, she was no longer there for me physically."

"I'm sorry, baby, I didn't know," Promise stated.

"No, its ok, I mean, I learned to deal with it over time but it was really rough back then. I literally had no family and when I turned thirteen, my moms passed away. One thing led to another and I found myself in a group home and being taken care of by the state. It was the loneliest, most depressing thing that I've ever had to endure. And it came at a time in my life, just before that transition time into my high school years and that was the time that I needed someone to lean on but there was just nobody there for me. It wasn't easy."

"What about your uncle?"

"Well, he had just finished doing like a 25 year bid so he didn't really have much to offer me. He was coming outta prison but he was coming home to nothing so what could he do for me? But I thank God for him because I always knew that he was like my ace in the hole that I could count on if things ever got rough or if I ever needed that 'big brother' protection.'"

"Yo, that is crazy, Audrey! So if I'm right, it's like you can sort of look at what you went through and project that on to Ashley. And you don't want Ashley to go through the same thing?"

"Exactly! Promise, her moms got killed and she can't help that. You're there for her but if something were to happen to you then she wouldn't be able to help that or help herself....The same way I couldn't help it that my mother got cancer and was taken from me. Growing up in a group home, it made me feel cheap and worthless and I just can't describe the feeling of feeling unwanted and unloved. But, at the same time, I knew that God is real because I would pray to him every night when I was in that group home and I would ask him to find me a home and find me a new mother and things like that. And so..."

Promise knew where I was going and he finished off my words, "Oh, so you're adopted?"

"Yup. And I don't know if you know all of the emotional baggage and issues that adopted kids and foster kids go through but it is no cakewalk. At age fifteen, I was really fortunate 'cause I was far from being a cute cuddly baby that most families adopt but, against all odds, I was adopted by the lady that you now hear me refer to as mom."

"That's wild," Promise stated, "I guess that we all have a story and we all have that unpaved road that we had to travel at one time or another."

"You right about that but we gotta make sure that little girl sitting back there doesn't have to travel down no unpaved roads," I said as I turned and glanced at Ashley who had fallen asleep with her Happy Meal toy placed nice and snug underneath her right arm.

****

We'd finally reached our destination of Hampton, Virginia and we decided to check into a hotel that wasn't too far from Hampton University. Promise and I both were exhausted. Poor little Ashley was knocked out and dead to the world. When we reached our room, I plopped myself on one of the two queen size beds and, if I had allowed myself to, I could have fallen fast asleep in under a minute. Promise woke Ashley up so that she could use the bathroom and then he tucked her into the bed.

"You hungry?" Promised asked.

"Nah, I'm good. I can wait until the morning to eat. We should go to the Waffle House for breakfast."

"A'ight, we'll do that."

When Promise and I were done with the small talk, we both undressed and decided to take a shower together. Not until I was undressing did it hit me that I didn't have a toothbrush, pajamas, slippers, a change of clothes, or even an extra pair of panties for that matter. I spoke my thoughts to Promise and he assured me that we would all go shopping in the morning to get some new gear and purchase some of life's essentials like toothbrushes and deodorant.

While we were in the shower, we both took turns lathering one another up with soap. Despite all of the hectic events that had been transpiring, it hadn't caused Promise to lose his touch. He had hands of gold and as he massaged my back, he caused chills to run up and down my body. I turned around and we both kissed while the water ran down our faces and our bodies. It felt so good to just experience Promise in a sexual and passionate way and I made sure to block out all of the thoughts about him being a cop killer, a bank robber, and a thug. Those thoughts were easy to block out considering that Promise soon had his *magic stick* inside of me and we were making love, doggystyle, right there in the shower. Usually, I'm the loud screaming type when I have sex but I knew that Ashley was in the other room so I had to try real hard to control my passionate feelings of ecstasy.

Promise and I went at if for like fifteen minutes in the shower and I wanted him to *shoot a double feature* but at the same time, I knew that we really couldn't enjoy ourselves the way we wanted to so I had to take what I could get when I could get it and not be greedy.

As we dried off our bodies and made it back into the bedroom of our hotel room, I hugged Promise's naked body and kissed him on the lips and said, "Baby, I just wish that we could do nothing but make love all day long."

"Tell me about it," Promise said as he gripped both of my butt checks and scooped me up off the ground. As he held me up in the air and against his hard chocolate body, I wrapped both of my legs around him and before kissing me, Promise looked me in my eyes and he assured me by saying, "One day, this whole 'on the run' thing is gonna be behind us. Trust me, it won't be too much longer before we get past all of this. You got my word about that. And when this is all over, I'm gonna go to Jacob The Jeweler and ice that ring finger for you. After that, we're gonna fly to Hawaii and get married on the beach."

I didn't respond to Promise. I just held onto him and hoped that his wishful thinking would one day come to pass. The two of us eventually made it into the bed. We didn't even bother to turn on the T.V. as we just laid in the dark and cuddled under the sheets together. I was thinking about saying a silent prayer and then going to sleep but just as I was about to pray, Promise's words interrupted me. And while he would eventually sleep like a baby for the rest of the night, it was his words, or his request of me that would keep me awake tossing and turning like a colicky baby until I finally willed myself to sleep for the night.

"Audrey, I know some people that I can hook up with that stay down here near Norfolk State University. And I got a plan that could get us some money and give us some breathing room for a while."

I didn't want to say anything that might burst Promise's bubble but I knew that whatever he was devising, it had to be something that was illegal. I kept quiet and just let him talk.

"See, it's a lot of cats from New York that moved down here to hustle. And I could stake out them cats and rob them but I don't think that would be the right move to make. I know that if I can get up some money, I can have you travel back to New York, make a purchase for me, and bring back some product and have these cats move it for me."

I knew that the "purchase" that Promise was talking about more than likely had something to do with illegal white powder. But I continued to remain silent as I was trying to figure out exactly what to say to Promise so that he would see the fruitlessness mentality that his lust for crime had him trapped in.

Promise continued on, "You seen how easy it was for me to get that money from that bank, right?"

"Um hmm," I said.

"Well, they got a whole lot of ECSB branches down here in Virginia. And the reason that the ECSB branches are a good target is because none of their branches have bulletproof partitions that separate the bank teller from the customers. So, if they get passed a note then they are more likely to go with the demands of the note because they know that they got nothing at all protecting them from potentially getting shot at point blank range."

Hoping that Promise would just hurry up and get to the punch line, I simply added another "Um hmm."

He continued on, "See, I figure that if we hit like three more branches and get about twenty thousand between the three then we would be good because I know I could flip that real quick. But, baby, what I need is, I need you to go in and pass the note to the tellers for me."

There was the punch line that I had been waiting for. I finally spoke up. "Promise, I don't know. I mean I got your back, you know that, but I don't think I can pull that off and plus, we ain't gotta do that. I can hold us down. I can get a job and take care of us."

Getting ready to try his hardest to convince me and sell me on his plot, Promise sat up and reached over to the nightstand and turned on the lamp, which caused both of our eyes to squint.

"Come on, baby, just three notes. That's all you gotta do. Pass three notes for me and we're good! I wanna take care of you. I don't want you taking care of me. I just need your help on this! You know I would have no problem doing it, but its just that my mugshot is about to be all over the place in a minute and it would be too risky for me to try anything. But if we hit three branches in the same day, back to back to back, then we'll be good. It won't take us more than like three hours, if that! Nothing is gonna go wrong baby. Trust me."

I buried my face in my hands as my heart began to race. And all I could think about was the last thing that my birth mother ever taught me and she taught me this on her deathbed. In fact, it's the last thing that she ever read to me and it comes from the Bible in 1 Cornithians 15:33. I could actually see and hear my mother reading those words that say, *"Do not be misled: Bad company corrupts good character."*

When my mother knew that she would be leaving this earth, she told me that there would be many things that she wished she could be around to guide me in but being that she was sick, she told me that I would have to rely on and trust God to guide me so that I would always do the right thing. She made sure though that she stressed to me that even if I trusted God to guide me, at times in life I would be faced with peer pressure type situations and in those situations I would need to remember the words of that scripture so that I would not follow the crowd and do wrong simply for the sake of doing what others want me to do, or for the sake of wanting to be accepted by others.

Trying to not get pinned down into making any stupid decisions, I said, "Promise, turn out the light. Lets just both get some sleep and in the morning, we'll talk about this."

"Nah, baby, I just wanna know," Promise said sounding like a spoiled child.

"You love me, right?" he asked.

"Promise, don't go there."

"OK, well then it's done. After we leave the Waffle House in the morning, we'll get ourselves two Nextel's and then we'll stop at the mall and get some clothes and all of the other stuff that we need. And when we're there, we'll make sure to buy you like three different pair of shades and three different hats so when you go in to the banks, you'll have three separate looks that won't give away your identity."

I didn't respond to Promise, partly because I was tired as hell and partly because I was trying to figure out how, without my consent, had Promise just *volunteered* me to rob banks for him? I was also thinking about the words from the Bible that my birth mother had spoken to me on her deathbed. I glanced over at Ashley and just the quick sight of her had influence on me so I sunk my body deeper into the mattress and pulled the covers over my head.

"Go to sleep, Promise," I instructed, "And turn out that light."

Promise did as I said and as he spooned me in the dark, I was trying my hardest to will myself to sleep. He didn't say anything else to me but I could tell that his mind was racing a mile a minute plotting and scheming.

****

As the three of us sat and ate breakfast at the Waffle House, I commented to Promise how I thought that one of the waitresses looked and sounded a lot like the character "Flo" from that hit TV show, *Alice*, from back in the late seventies and early eighties. "Flo" was the one with the accent that would always yell at her boss Mel and tell him to "Kiss her grits!"

At first, Promise didn't know what TV show that I was talking about but when it finally hit him, he agreed with me that the waitress in fact did have a striking resemblance to "Flo." So, as we sat and ate Promise spoke to the white lady and asked her did anyone ever tell her that she looks like "Flo."

"Oh, I get that all the time, baby. If I had a dollar for everyone that told me that then I would be rich."

Promise and I both chuckled, while Ashley seemed as if she didn't have a clue as to what was so funny. Little did we know that Promise had just sparked the talkative juices in our waitress - Flo.

"So, where are y'all from? Y'all sound like y'all from New York City," Flo said with a big bright smile as she commented how cute Ashley was.

At that point, Promise and I began to fumble over our words. At the exact same time, I blurted out that *we* were from Long Island and he blurted out that *we* were from Pennsylvania. Flo looked at us with a confused look on her face. I realized that Promise was more than likely trying to protect our identities so I quickly made an attempt to clean up my slip of the tongue.

"Well, we are originally from Long Island but we moved to Allentown, Pennsylvania about five years ago. I guess we just never lost our New York accents."

Flo smiled and said that she could recognize a New York accent in a heartbeat.

"Yeah, I used to live in Brooklyn years ago."

"Really?" I chimed in.

"Yeah, I used to live in Coney Island right down the block from the amusement park but that was way back in the late sixties, probably before you guys were even born."

Under the table, Promise nudged my leg trying to get me to shut the heck up so that the conversation with Flo could end. I took the hint and I realized that too much running of the mouth was definitely no good because if Promise's face just happened to show up on TV, or on some wanted posters, or in the newspapers then holding conversations with people like "Flo" would do nothing but help to jar their memory at a later date.

Flo eventually went to serve other customers and that gave me and Promise some time to engage in conversation with each other. I guess from a distance that Flo could see that we were talking about something that appeared to be private, so aside from asking us if could she get anything else for us, she kept quiet from there on out.

I was glad that she had left us alone because Promise had begun to talk about me renting an apartment in my name as quickly as possible so that we could get up out of that money-draining hotel that we were in. We spoke about that at length and we agreed that in a few days that I would do just that, in terms of using my name and my good credit rating to secure us an apartment some where in the Newport News neighborhood.

Before long, we had made it out of the Waffle House and had made our way over to the mall. Promise held true to his word and after buying some toys and candy for Ashley he purchased about five outfits for each of us. He also made sure to purchase the necessary essentials for us like toothpaste and deodorant. Being that I had discarded my phone as had Promise, we also purchased two Nextel's.

Promise was like most men in that while I wanted to shop and browse and go in and out of stores, he wanted to get in the mall and get the hell out as quickly as possible. Not that he was worried about protecting his identity; it was just that he hated "shopping like a god-damn woman" as he so eloquently put it.

By about 12 noon, we had made it back to our hotel room. Ashley was drained from all of the running around and she headed straight for the bed so that she could lay down. Promise proceeded to place his large wad of cash inside of the small safe that was in the closet. And while I put the new clothes on hangers and inside the dresser drawers, Promise turned on the TV and began to flip channels.

He stopped channel surfing when he reached CNN Headline News. Both of our mouths dropped as we watched and listened as they reported on the New York City police officer that had been killed. But what really had caught us off guard, and I guess we should have seen it coming, was when they flashed a mug-shot of Promise.

"Daddy!" Ashley shouted with joy as she quickly sat up, smiled and pointed to the TV and shouted, "Daddy's on TV!"

Little did she know that by her daddy being *on TV* was in no way a good thing. Not wanting his daughter to see him on TV in that fashion, Promise quickly turned the channel.

"See, Audrey, that's why I didn't want you running your mouth the way you were with that 'Flo' waitress!"

In my head, I could not believe that Promise had just snapped at me with the tone in which he had used. I wanted to blurt out and tell him that he needed to check his short-term memory and realize that it was his ass that had started the conversation with the lady.

"Promise, why are you snapping at me?"

"Because you were running your mouth when all you had to do was sit there and eat!"

I knew that Promise was frustrated and agitated because he had just seen his cover blown on national television but I couldn't just sit there and get blamed for something that wasn't even my fault.

"Hold up a minute, baby! I know that you're stressed out and all but it was you, not me, you who started the whole conversation with that waitress in the first place. So. don't try to put this off on me!"

"Oh, so you're blaming this all on me?"

"Promise, I'm not blaming nothing on you. All I'm saying is that I barely said anything to the woman! You are the one that spoke up and spoke first to 'Flo.'"

"Well, what the hell was all of that *'we're from Long Island?'*. What the hell did you say that for?"

"Ok Promise, look. I can see that this ain't going anywhere. And what's done is done so if you want me to take the blame then fine, I'll take the blame!"

"What!?"

"What do you mean, what!?"

"I'm sayin', why are you all of a sudden trying to disrespect my ass!?"

"Promise, what are you talking about? Ain't nobody trying to disrespect you. Look, obviously you are just stressed out because of everything that's going on and I understand that so lets just drop the whole thing."

"Nah, I'm not dropping a got damn thing!"

I couldn't believe that I was seeing a side of Promise that I had never seen before. I guess he is the type that cracks under the pressure. I was also wondering if my uncle Brandon had intuitively sensed something about Promise that I had failed to see as a warning signal.

As Ashley pleaded for her daddy and I to not yell at each other, Promise continued on, "I'm not dropping nothing! I see your little pattern! *First you talk all slick* and then you just wanna *drop* everything!"

"Promise, what in the hell are you talking about me talking 'slick'? Are you trying to call me a snake?"

"Oh, see now you're gonna play stupid! No, I'm not calling you a snake! You know exactly what I'm talking about!"

I could not believe that this utterly ridiculous argument was taking place.

"No, Promise, I *really* don't know what you are talking about! So tell me, what are you talking about!?"

"Last night, that little stunt that you pulled. I was talking to you and practically pouring my heart out to you and asking you for a favor. And it's like I'm vulnerable right now and you know I need you but your ass chose to ignore me and just go to sleep! In essence, you just wanted to *drop* the subject just like now you wanna *drop it*! I'm just waiting for you to *drop me*! Matter of fact, I'm not begging your ass for nothing. If you wanna drop me and drop everything, then do that! You can take the car keys, get in the car, and head your ass back to New York right now!"

"Okay, okay... Whoa! Whoa! Wait a minute. Lets just please slow everything down for a minute," I said as I looked at Promise and I couldn't believe that he really looked vexed!

"Promise, you're saying that you asked me for a favor, a favor as if you ask someone to borrow some milk or something. But that wasn't the kind of favor that you asked of me. You asked me to rob a bank for crying out loud! Three banks at that! Maybe it's just me but that is a whole helluva lot bigger than a *favor*!"

Promise remained quiet and he didn't say anything. He simply started popping the tags off of some of his new gear and began getting dressed. When he was done getting dressed, he did the same for his daughter.

"Before you head back to New York, can you just do me one more solid and I won't ask you for anything else. It's not the apartment. I'll figure out how to take care of that... All I want you to do is just take me and Ashley to a car rental place and rent a car for us. That's it! You can keep the

BMW. I gave your uncle my word that it would be your car and I'm sticking to my word. Plus, by you keeping the car that will be like my payment to you for all that you've done for me."

I didn't know if Promise was playing with my head or if he was dead serious but I did know that he was good at manipulating my feelings.

"Promise, I'm not leaving your side."

"Audrey, forget it! Just like you've been saying to me, *just drop it*. We'll be a'ight. I'll get up this money and me and my daughter will be a'ight."

Promise was really convincing me that he was in fact serious. I wanted to request that he at least let me take Ashley back to New York with me but I doubted that he would go for that.

All of a sudden, I remember wondering and thinking to myself that Promise really must have been spoiled as a kid or something because he had managed to deflect everything off of himself. He spun things in such a way where he was making me feel guilty for not enabling his ways. He was coming across as if he was the victim or something.

As much as I didn't want to do it and knowing that it would be going against my mother's deathbed advice, I began to put on one of my new outfits. I put on one of the hats that I had purchased along with my shades. Promise looked at me and I know that he had no clue what I was preparing for but he kept quiet.

"Pass me my bag, baby," I instructed, "and hand me the car keys too."

Promise did as I instructed.

"Look, its just about 12:30. We already wasted enough time. Now, if we're gonna hit these three banks before they close at three o'clock then we need to hurry up and lets do this," I said. I could not believe the words that were coming out of my mouth.

Suddenly, like a kid who had been told that he was off of punishment, Promise's whole demeanor sprang to life. He approached me with a huge smile plastered across his face. As he hugged me, he spoke into my ear and said, "Thank you so much baby!"

I shot right back, "Promise, we don't have time for all of this hugging. Lets just hurry up and do this before I change my mind."

"Okay, okay," Promise said as he scrambled around the room to retrieve my other pairs of shades and my other hats as he prepared for us to depart and do our dirt.

Before departing, Promise did manage to sit me down at the table that was in our room and he had me construct the three separate notes that I would pass to the tellers. He also went over some last minute logistics so that I would know and be clear on just exactly what it was that I needed to do.

When my quick tutorial was over, Promise placed his loaded silver hand gun inside my bag and told me that I wouldn't need to use it but that it would be there at my disposal just in case I had to scare or really threaten 'some clown ass that might try to flex' as he put it.

Ashley, Promise, and myself quickly left the hotel room. After Ashley was strapped into her booster seat, Promise and I headed towards our first destination. As we drove, we talked and both agreed that we would check out of the hotel as soon as we were done hitting the banks. Things would probably be way too hot to stay in that same hotel.

****

As usual, I did the driving so that if we were ever stopped by the cops, chances would be that only my driver's license would be checked. And unlike Promise, I didn't have any warrants out for my arrest so with a clean record it made logical sense for me to be doing all of the driving.

Promise didn't want to use one of our new Nextel's so he had me stop at a pay phone so that he could call information. He got the number to ECSB customer service and called them for the addresses to the branches that were located in the Hampton Road area.

"There's a branch right near the Coliseum Mall and that's not too far from here," Promise stated as he got back in the car.

I have to admit that at that point my heart was racing so fast and my palms were so sweaty that I couldn't even think straight. I barely understood or heard Promise as he was instructing me on how to get to the mall.

"Audrey, you ok?"

"Yeah, I'm good. I'm just nervous as hell!"

"Don't worry. It's gonna be easy. Just pass the note to the teller, that's all. It'll be just like passing her a withdrawal slip," Promise re-explained in an attempt to ease my fears.

"I'll be ok. It's just that in my wildest dreams, I never ever thought that I would be doing something like this! Word!"

We reached the parking lot of the Coliseum Mall and thankfully, the bank was not actually inside the main part of the mall itself. The bank stood alone and it was about a good one hundred yards or so from the mall. So, rather than walk the hundred yards, I navigated my way through the parked cars until I reached the bank.

"You ready?" Promise asked as I pulled the car into a parking space behind the bank.

"Yeah, I'm ready."

I didn't say another word as I mentally prepped and prepared myself to go through with this bold criminal act that could easily land my ass in a federal prison if I were to get caught.

Ashley broke my concentration as she spoke up and asked, "Ms. Audrey, can I come with you inside the bank? Please."

"No, sweetie," I responded, "Just sit here with your daddy, I'll be right back."

I exited the car. The walk to the bank felt like it was taking forever! My legs felt like a ton of bricks. My mouth was as dry as an Arizona desert. My palms were so sweaty that I was afraid that I might smudge the ink on the note that I had to pass to the teller.

When I entered the bank, I noticed everything and everyone. It seemed as if all eyes were on my black ass. I slowly made my way over to a counter and pretended as if I was filling out a deposit slip. Although it was just in my head, I really felt like everyone was looking at me, customers and all, and that just furthered my extreme anxiety.

Being that it was Friday afternoon, the bank was somewhat crowded but thank God – if I can even thank God in a situation like this – but thank God that the line for business customers only had one person standing in line at the time.

I got behind that one business customer and that customer was soon called. My heart really began to pound and I knew that it was now or never. 'Audrey, just turn around and get your ass up out of this bank! Girl are you crazy!

What are you even doing in here?' I asked myself. 'You ain't no bank robber!' I tried to remind myself.

The customer ahead of me seemed as if she was taking way too long. *They had to know something was up. They had to know what I was preparing to do. Maybe they signaled for the cops to come and were trying to stall me until the cops got here.* As all of those thoughts ran through my head the teller finally finished with her customer and she very pleasantly said, "Hello, you can step forward."

With my powder blue Roc-a-wear sweat suit on and my S. Carter sneakers, I stepped forward. My dark shades hid my eyes in a mysterious kind of way but with the hat that I was wearing, it allowed the shades to naturally flow with everything else in my outfit and I simply looked like some hip-hop chick. The only thing that was out of place was my Burberry bag because it didn't match my outfit at all but that was a very small and minor detail.

I made it to the teller. She looked so much like Britney Spears, it was amazing! Somehow with my mouth now drier that an eighty year old vagina, I managed to smile a genuine smile. I don't know where I mustered up the smile but it seemed to have took a whole lot of tension out of my body.

The Britney Spears looking teller smiled back at me and asked, "How can I help you?"

Hoping that I didn't look nervous, I exhaled and I tried to run a little game as best I could. "I know that people must tell you all the time that you look like Britney Spears," I said to the teller as I reached my hand inside the Burberry bag and gripped the gun.

"I get that all the time," the teller acknowledged.

"Well, take it as a compliment. I mean, after all, Britney is a pretty girl." I don't know why on earth I had said that because I didn't want that chick to think that I was hitting on her.

"Oh, thank you for the compliment," she gleefully replied.

I was thinking that the small talk was over and it was time to hand her the note and I did just that. I made sure that I also placed the Burberry bag onto the counter top and I kept my right hand inside the bag. The gun was literally pointed at the teller and my finger was on the trigger. "Britney" as I like to call her, read the note that said:

-This is not a game! The handbag that you see on the counter has a loaded gun and it is pointed directly at your head! Place a large quantity of large bills inside an envelope for me and pass me the envelope. Don't panic and don't look alarmed and don't alert anyone and no one will get hurt. –

After reading the note, "Britney" looked up at me with a "deer in the headlights" kind of way. I simply gave her one of those uppity, sophisticated, diva smiles and I commented under my breath. "This ain't a game! Hurry up!"

My heart was pounding. As nervous as I was, I could now see and understand how Promise had pulled the trigger and shot that cop in the heat of the moment because, at that present moment in time, I was scared that my nerves might cause me to accidentally pull the trigger and pop the teller for no reason.

"Britney" did as the note had instructed and she handed me a letter size envelope that was stuffed with cash. I looked inside the envelope real quick and confirmed that there were large bills inside. I didn't say thank you and I just turned around and quickly walked out of the bank. I wanted to run but I didn't want to bring any attention to myself. I was so nervous that I didn't even breathe until I got to the car.

When I got to the car the car's engine was running. I opened the driver's door and handed the money to Promise. I finally allowed myself to breathe. Dramatically exhaling, I said, "Promise, that was the scariest thing that I ever did in my life!"

"But you did it, baby! Yes! That's what I talking about! That's my girl right there!"

It felt good to hear Promise cheering me on but I was more concerned about how to quickly navigate up out of that parking lot. Promise directed me and we were quickly off to our next spot.

While we drove, Promise wanted to know all of the details of what transpired inside the bank but my nerves were still on edge and I wasn't in the frame of mind to talk. I just wanted to hurry up and get the other two robberies over with.

The second ECSB branch was about two or three miles away and we reached it in no time. It was located on a relatively busy boulevard called Mercury Boulevard.

"Promise, don't take my silence as disrespect or anything but I just wanna stay in my *zone* until we get this over with."

Promise understood. As I put on a lighter shade pair of sunglasses and a different color hat, Promise suggested that I take off the top half of the sleeveless sweat suit that I was wearing. Even though we had just *hit* the other bank, he didn't want to take the chance that a description of what I had been wearing was broadcast to the other banks in the area.

His suggestion was good and it proved my theory that in crime type situations, there is always a calm person that can think logically and that person is usually not perpetrator of the crime, the one with the adrenaline flowing rapidly throughout their body.

So after taking heed to Promise's suggestion, I took off the sweat suit top and I made my way into the second bank. I was wearing a white tube top and being that my breast are very large, the tube top did a very poor job of containing those two bad boys. My nipples were protruding through the tube top like two huge Del Monte raisins, not to mention that I had cleavage showing for days!

I knew that since I had just hit the other bank that I couldn't waste anytime fiddling around inside this particular branch. I headed straight for the teller lines, not stopping at the counter to pretend to fill out a deposit slip or anything like that. Ironically, the line for business customers was quite long and the line for regular customers was short. I took a calculated chance and just got on the line for regular customers.

The reason that I say calculated is because it looked as if the white male teller was ready to call the next customer and I was desperately hoping that he would take me first before calling one of the business customers to his regular line to be helped. My calculated move paid off and the late twenty something white male signaled for me to come to his line.

Everyone knows that white guys love themselves some big titties in the same way that black guys love big butts. I had purposely wanted to get the teller that had called me because I wanted to try and distract him with my protruding boobs.

When I reached his teller station, I made sure that I relaxed my handbag and my entire right arm on the counter so that the bottom of the handbag was facing the teller. But I also made sure that I visibly rested my tube topped titties right there on the counter so that they were practically spilling out on to the counter. It looked as if I was serving them up on a platter or something. The white guy smiled and he couldn't help but look at my chest.

"So, how are you doing today?" I asked. I wanted the white guy to think that I was flirting with him.

"I'm doing fine and yourself?" He said as his blue eyes were glued to my chest.

"Not bad but I'm kind of in a hurry."

"Oh, ok, so how can I help you?"

"Well, I wanna make a withdrawal," I said as I passed him the note.

Before he finished reading the note, I spoke up under my breath in an attempt to speed things up.

"Baby, this is not a joke so just hurry up!" I said as I removed my titties from the counter top so that he wouldn't be distracted. I made sure to keep my hand on the trigger inside my handbag and the handbag still on the counter top, pointed in the teller's direction.

In no time, the teller had complied with my demands and he handed me a stuffed envelope. I didn't look inside the envelope. I simply said "thank you" and I turned and made my way out of the bank and back into the car.

Unlike the previous parking lot, Mercury Boulevard was the perfect boulevard for a get away because in a matter of seconds, I was driving and in the mix with the rest of the other cars. As I pulled off, I exhaled and I handed the envelope full of loot to Promise.

"That was actually much easier that time," I informed Promise.

"It's all down hill baby after the first one," Promise explained with a huge sparkling smile plastered across his face.

Promise directed me towards our third and final bank location. As we drove, I was in more of a mood to talk. Sounding very animated, I stated, "Baby, that last one was so funny! I had to go with my gut instincts and I didn't get on the business line. I just got on the regular line because the business line was more crowded. So there was this white teller. He looked like he was about twenty-seven or twenty-eight years old. I walked up to his teller station and propped my titties right up on the counter and it was so funny because I could tell that he was drooling over me! That was probably the closest that he ever came to some dark meat in his life. So, while I had him drooling, I slipped him the note and he didn't know what to think. So, I was like 'baby, this is not joke so just hurry up!' Yo, homeboy handed me that money so quick! Oh, it was so funny 'cause his blue eyes was so wide open and I know he couldn't believe that he was getting got the way he was!"

Promise laughed and he commented how I was real smooth with mine. Then he told me that he had counted the loot from the first bank and that there was a little over eight grand in the envelope.

"Eight grand!?" I asked in astonishment.

"Yup."

"Damn, I guess crime does pay," I joked.

Promise and I both began laughing. We were quickly approaching the last branch and Promise stated, "Okay Audrey, this is the last one. Just do exactly like you did on the other two. Get in and get out as quick as you can. And remember that the third time is always the charm so just relax and stay calm."

When I reached the last branch that was located not too far from Rip Rack Road, on a street called Settler's

Landing, right near Hampton University, I told Promise that I think I needed to completely take off the hat and the shades just in case all of the banks were hip to my M.O.

"Nah, keep on the shades. Don't worry about the hat but what you do is this, here, wear my t-shirt," Promise said as he began taking off his shirt. "It'll look over-sized on you but that's a'ight because it is a completely different color. You had on all light colors before and this shirt is black so you should be good."

I took Promise's t-shirt and put it on over my tube top while Promise sat in the car with his wife beater on. Just in case, if someone had seen us leaving one of the previous banks, we decided to park in a gas station that was right near the third bank. The last thing we wanted was the cops or anyone else catching us out there because of the car that we were in.

I have to admit that I was contemplating not going forward with the third robbery. I mean Promise had damn near five thousand dollars in the closet safe back at the hotel. I had taken more than eight grand from the first bank that I hit. So right there was thirteen grand that we had accumulated and we hadn't even counted the money from second bank! In my heart, I just felt that we didn't have to risk hitting the last bank but I was afraid to speak up because we were on such a roll and so far, there had been no hitches in the plan that Promise had devised. There was really no need to start doubting him. But, in all honesty, I was also thinking that maybe Promise should hit the last bank simply because if all of the banks were hip to me by now then they would more than likely have all of their employees on the lookout for a suspicious looking black female, not a black male.

We were in the gas station parking lot and my heart began to rapidly pump gallons of nervous blood through my body. I never spoke up about the reservations that I had. I figured that hitting the last bank was like taking medicine and I need not complain. I just needed to do what I had to do and get it over with.

Something just didn't feel right though and I could tell that Promise also had some doubts about our chances of success on the last bank. I say that because as I was stepping out of the car, Promise says to me, "Yo, if anything don't look right on my end I'll get in the driver's seat and I'll key you on the Nextel but I won't say anything. So, if you hear that 'bloop-bloop' sound coming from your Nextel, that'll mean that something is up and I want you to get your ass back to the car as fast as you can with or without the loot. Okay?"

"Okay," I said as I shut the door to the BMW and fearfully made my way into the bank.

****

When I entered the third bank, things just seemed very eerie and surreal. It was sort of as if things were moving in slow motion. I scanned the bank with my eyes and I noticed that this bank was the most crowded of the three that I had entered.

I made my way to the counter in order to fake like I was filling out a withdrawal slip and that's when I noticed that there was a security guard standing near one of the teller locations.

'Audrey, get your ass up out of this bank right now! They gotta know what's up,' I told myself. I didn't hesitate and I quickly made my way back to the car.

"That was quick," Promise stated.

"They had a security guard standing right near one of the tellers! Things just don't seem right, Promise."

"Don't sweat that, baby. All banks usually have a security guard or something. But I guarantee you that he wasn't holding no heat! He ain't nothing but a toy-cop, an unarmed security guard."

"I don't know, Promise."

"Come on, baby, just get it over with. Matter of fact, I'll tell you what. Give me the note and I'll just add on the note that the teller better not alarm the security guard."

I shook my head and thought about things for a couple of minutes. After a minute or two, I decided to just go along with everything. I exited the car and made my way back inside the bank. My heart was beating so fast that I thought it was gonna jump out of my shirt. By the time that I had made it back inside the bank, the security guard had re-positioned himself and he was now standing near the entrance / exit doors of the bank.

I blocked everything out of my mind and I stood on the long commercial line. As I waited on the line, what I did was I just thought about how good it would feel to go home and sleep in my own bed and just relax and end all of the drama that I was putting myself through. I thought about things like that so that I wouldn't psych myself out of going through with the robbery.

'Audrey, when this is over, we're checking out of that hotel. You are renting an apartment for Promise and then you are taking your ass back to New York! No more of this *gangster's girl* nonsense!' I told myself, 'If anything, I'll just make a pact with Promise that if something ever happens to him, that I will do whatever it is that I have to do to get custody of his daughter. I'll be there for him in that way but I can't ride with him any longer in the manner in which I'm riding with him.'

Finally, after about fifteen minutes of waiting, I reached the teller. The teller was a middle aged white lady and the moment that she saw me, I could sense that she probably had been alerted to lookout for someone that fit my description. I say that because both of her eyes immediately shifted to the right side of her head and she began acting fidgety and nervous. Most likely, she was probably thinking back to a description that her boss had given her of me, the New York bred Hampton Roads bank robber.

Without speaking any words of "hello" or anything like that, I passed the teller the note. I put my handbag on the counter with my hand inside the bag and my finger on the gun's trigger.

"I know that they probably told you to be on the lookout for me. And I know that you know who I am. So just play everything cool and calm and do what the note says."

The lady read the note and immediately her face went pale and she looked flustered as if she had just seen a ghost.

"Oh my God. Oh my God! This is not happening. I can not believe this is happening!" The lady began saying.

Under my breath, I spoke in the sternest tone that I could muster up. I spoke with my teeth clinched tightly together and I said, "Lady, if you do what the note says I will not hurt you! You gotta do this quick 'cause I don't have all day!" Little did the teller know that I was probably more scared than she was.

I quickly took my eyes off of her and I glanced to see what the security guard was doing and as I figured, he was looking right in my direction. Fortunately for me, the teller was carrying out the demands of the note as the guard suspiciously looked on.

"Just one more second, please just give me one more second," the teller begged.

"Stop talking and hurry up!" I barked with my teeth stilled clinched together.

As the teller handed me the envelope, I noticed that one of the other tellers was looking closely at what was going on.

'She had to have tripped some alarm or something,' I told myself referring to the nosy teller that had suddenly begun to scope things out a bit too closely.

I knew that I had to move very rapidly and get out of that bank. There had been nothing smooth about the third robbery and I just wanted to make it back to the hotel so that I could tell Promise that my mission had been accomplished and that I would be heading back to New York. This would definitely be the end of the crime road for me.

As I prepared to walk past the security guard, I tightly gripped the envelope full of cash and my handbag both with my left hand. Out of force of habit, if I am walking to my car, I always reach for my car keys before I actually get to the car. So due to my nervousness as well as force of habit, I began searching in my pocket for the car keys. Totally forgetting that the car keys were still in the car, I began to panic because I was thinking that I had misplaced the keys. I frantically reached into my pocket a second time and that's when I remembered that the keys were still in the car's ignition.

Realizing that I had made it past the security guard, I blew out some air from my lungs. As I reached to push open the door that led outside the bank. The security guard spoke up and said to me, "Uhm excuse me."

Not knowing what to do, I stopped dead in my tracks but I did not turn around and look at him.

'God damn! I'm busted!' I screamed at myself. "Just go, Audrey, just go!" I urged myself but I was literally paralyzed with fear and I remained still.

Then the security guard sounded as if he was heading in my direction and he began to speak again only this time he spoke more assertively, "Excuse me Ms.! I think you dropped..."

As the security guard was in the middle of saying what he was saying, my paralysis had suddenly left me and I reached my hand inside of the hand bag and grabbed the gun and, without thinking, I spun and pulled the trigger all in one motion.

I caught the unarmed security guard with a hot one right in his stomach. The sound of the bullet discharging from the gun was tremendous! The security guard fell to the ground writhing and screaming in pain as something fell out of his hand. At that point, all hell broke loose as people inside the bank began yelling and screaming and ducking for cover.

I turned back around and violently pushed open the bank doors trying to get the hell out of dodge as quick as I could and in the process, I knocked down a customer that was on their way inside the bank. Like a track star, I sprinted to the BMW and I jumped in the driver's seat as I was screaming hysterically.

"Oh my God! Promise! Promise! Promise! I shot somebody! I shot the security guard!" I screamed as I literally trembled with fear.

"What!? What happened?" Promise asked.

"I don't know! I panicked and I just turned and shot the security guard without thinking!"

As I continued to just shake with fear, Promise yelled at me to forget about what had happened and for me to just get hit the gas pedal and drive.

"Drive!" He screamed as we both heard sirens coming from every direction.

I didn't know where I was going as I weaved my way onto different roads. I actually saw cops speeding by me as they apparently were making their way to the ECSB branch that I had just hit. Before I knew what was what, I realized that I was on I-64 and somewhat in the clear.

"Promise, I can't do this anymore! I gotta get back to New York! I can't keep doing this!"

"Okay, okay, baby. I understand. Just get back to the hotel and we'll check out and then we'll sort everything out," Promise stated as he attempted to calm my fears.

"No, baby, I don't think you understand me. I just have to leave now! I can't wait around and help you get an apartment or anything like that down here I just gotta go! The cops are after *me* now! I can't believe this!"

Promise tried his best to calm my fears and he told me that he would more than likely troop back with me to New York and try to get in touch with Squeeze and Show and hide out up in the Bronx somewhere.

While he spoke, Promise did convince me to make one last stop back at the hotel. I mean actually there were about five thousand reasons for him to desperately wanna make the stop back at the hotel so I didn't go against his wishes. But I really just wanted to just get up out of Virginia and get on I-95 and head north, *like yesterday!*

With my heart still pounding and my nerves ready to explode out of my body, I said, "Promise, be in and out! Don't go to the checkout desk or nothing. Just get the money out of the safe, grab those clothes, and let's get up outta here!"

Promise agreed.

We pulled into the parking lot of the hotel and Promise quickly jumped out of the car and headed to our room.

"Ms. Audrey, what's the matter?" Ashley so innocently asked.

"Oh, nothing, baby. I was just scared about something, sweetie," I said to Ashley as I tried my best to come across as if I was in control of the situation. "but don't worry, everything is gonna be ok. We'll get you some McDonald's real soon. Okay, sweetie?"

"Ok," Ashley replied.

At that point, I just closed my eyes for a five seconds and I tried to relax. With my eyes closed, I replayed the scene of me shooting the security guard. Then all of a sudden *it* hit me like a ton of brick! I realized what had happened inside the bank was that when I was exiting the bank and searching for my car keys, I must have dropped that credit card looking hotel room key that the hotels give you when you check in.

"Uggh!" I said to myself in anguish as I realized that my hotel room key had simply fallen out of my pocket when I was frantically searching for the car keys and the security guard was only trying to alert me to that fact. 'Audrey! How could you have been so stupid and panicked like that!?' When the guard had said 'Excuse me, Ms., I think you dropped...' he was more than likely telling me that I had dropped my hotel room key. Damn!"

I opened my eyes back up and I checked my pockets for my hotel room key and sure enough, it was not in my pocket. After checking my pockets, I noticed about four unmarked cars that looked like the type of cars that law enforcement would drive. Two of the cars were empty but as for the other two cars, they were not empty and four white men quickly piled out of the cars.

'That gotta be the police!' I told myself. 'They found the hotel key that fell out of the security guard's hand when he was trying to hand it back to me and they must have traced it back to this hotel! Ah man!'

I reached for my Nextel and I used the walkie-talkie feature and I urgently said, "Promise, forget the money! I really messed us up! We gotta bounce right now! Hurry up and come back to the car! Now! Hurry up!"

Promise hit me back and he sounded like he was running and out of breath or something as he yelled into his Nextel, "Baby, take Ashley and just go. Don't wait for me, just go!"

"Promise!" I yelled into the Nextel.

Promise came back on the Nextel and as he was yelling me to leave him and to just go and drive off without him, I could hear someone in the background screaming, "FBI freeze!"

I started up the car and peeled off in reverse.

Promise chimed back in on the Nextel, "Audrey!" he yelled and as he yelled, I heard a gun shot sound come through on the Nextel.

"Oh God!" I said to myself as I feared the worst.

I put the car in drive and as I was peeling off, the car suddenly began to fill up with this red misty looking substance. It looked as if someone was spraying some type of aerosol can full of red spray paint into the car.

Before I knew what was what, I couldn't see a thing and everything inside the car was red. Everything! I would later find out that the teller at the last bank had slipped what is called a *dye-pack* into the envelope along with the cash.

The dye-pack, like most dye-packs was on a timer and it got tripped when I walked out of the bank with stolen money, the same way a store alarm is tripped if you were to try to walk out of a store with stolen merchandise. Once the alarm was tripped, it activated a fifteen-minute timer that released the dye and stained the money and my clothes, Ashley's clothes, and the entire tan leather interior of the BMW. The dye-pack had done its job in that the money had become useless to me and to Promise for that matter being that it was now very recognizable *marked* money.

The next thing that I remember after the car filled up with red mist was that I crashed into something. I don't know what it was that I had crashed into because I couldn't see where I was going. Then I remember all four of the car doors being violently ripped open. I was suddenly yanked out of the car and rammed to the concrete pavement. I heard the sound of men and women yelling, "FBI, stay on the ground!"

I knew that at that point, a big chunk of my life if not my entire life was over but my thoughts were still with Ashley.

"There's a baby in the car!" I yelled.

"Shut the hell up!" One of the officers said as he jammed his size thirteen foot on the back of my head and neck area.

As my face lay on the concrete, I remember thinking about how painful the officer's boot was as it pressed in on the back of my neck and prevented me from breathing. I attempted to turn my head so that I could get a small bit of air into my lungs but in the process, all I managed to do was rip and tear the skin off the left side of my face as it scraped against the concrete. It was so bad that the white meat was showing.

My arms were then jerked and yanked behind me and twisted up like a chicken wing. At that point, I heard someone yell, "I got the baby!"

I wanted desperately to look and see what was going on with Ashley but I couldn't move. The officers and agents had put the cuffs so tight on my wrist that it actually felt like the cuffs had broken both of my wrists.

"Get up!" One of the FBI agents yelled as they continued to manhandle me and yanked me up off the concrete.

They escorted me to one of the unmarked cars. As I walked with an oversized T-Shirt which was stained with red-dye, my face was scraped, bleeding, and cut up, and my wrists were numb and stinging because of the cuffs that almost broke my wrist, I couldn't help but think over and over about the words from the Bible that my birth mother spoke to me on her death bed:

"Do not be misled: Bad company corrupts good character."

One block to go...
by: Anthony Whyte

Brooklyn, N.Y. --- *Pooh's Last Night*

I ran as hard as I could dodging bullets all the way. These people in front of me walking all slow better get outta my way. Running so hard, I could feel my heart pounding, my breath coming in gasps. I didn't see 'em but I knew I hadn't lost 'em just yet. Another block to go and I'll exit this place.

The whole scene reminded me of being chased by bullies through the school playground. I'm in spasms thinking of what to do next. Just when I thought I'd out run 'em and tried to hide, those on foot spotted me. There was hardly any traffic out this early so I ran in search of the subway. I wasn't punk'd either. I was just trying to make a getaway. Not caring, my body crashing into dope fiends. It's early morning and I'm knocking down ladies of the night as I skipped across the busy boulevard. Along with the fiends, they were only ones out.

"Where's the subway station?" I slowed and asked, breathing hard.

"One block ahead," was the response.

The reply was barely off someone's lips when suddenly there was a bright flash of headlights. I heard the screech of tires and the gunshots. I jumped over a baby carriage pushed by another fiend. Almost out of breath, I kept hitting the asphalt. I had to get the fuck up out this hood. I'd just made it past the bodega on the street corner. The only light I could see was the red and green glow from lamps next to the subway station.

I ran a couple more blocks then slowed a little to dip down the stairs of the station. Suddenly I realized how close on my heels they were to me. They had caught up with me. I stumbled and went rolling down the urine soaked stairs of the New Lots Ave subway line. Crawling on hands and knees trying to recover, all I heard was '*Bang! Bang! Bang!*' Three shots rang at once above the roar of the train. I felt the burn on my insides and smelt my flesh afire. Bullets crashed through to the bones under my clothes leaving my left thigh numb for a couple seconds. Everything became blurry as intense pain surged through to my brain.

Angry voices of threats hollowed as if I was trapped inside a time warp machine where the sounds doubled. Sweating hard and accelerating I was, but really only moving at a snail's crawl. This had to be repercussions from robbing Nine and his crew.

My lungs burned from grueling inhalations. I was determined not to die out here in these parts where no one knew me or my rep. I had to make it, call my boys. My homies, where were they? I don't wanna die. I ain't really lived yet, I kept telling myself.

My breath came in gasps. I could barely run but continued to struggle. Every move made was getting too painful for me to endure and the shells burned like hell. Sluggishly knowing that my luck was running out, I dragged on.

"Yeah asshole, what you got to say now? Huh, huh what? Huh? What you gonna do now? This is what you get for robbing my girl, you bi-yotch!" I heard the yelling and straining my neck I tried to peek at them. These cats chasing me weren't Nine and his crew like I'd thought.

"Yeah, fight like a man, coward! What, you too scared to fight a real man, huh? Yeah, but you ain't scared to rob a girl?" This threat was from another set tryin' to off me for jooksing down some broad. That's it? They hunting me for robbing a broad? What broad? For a moment, the thought swirled in my mind yet I couldn't remember. From behind a pile of subway trash, I could see three of them. They were all Spanish with mugs that showed no mercy. These clowns have got to be loco. This had to be some kinda crazy mix-up. I mean getting killed over a broad, these cats got to be furgazy!

"Yo man what girl I rob? I ain't robbed no broads..." I started to yell thinking I could buy time. As the words rolled off my tongue, the answer immediately struck me like a bullet to the head. I'd given up my position and they took aim with the answer.

"The bitch you robbed a couple of *weeks* ago, cocksucker, that's my sister. No one messes with my sis - You fuck with my family - you die." The rats began to stir *and* the noise caused a welcome distraction. I thought carefully for a minute while their backs were turned.

They could call me pussy, whatever, I wasn't gonna show out. I'd live to fight another day. Before running, the question of heart reared up. Was I scared to die? There was a definite struggle between being brave and a coward. At the same time, my heart was telling me to turn around and fight to the end. I'd give it a thought then a spray of bullets jumpstarted my efforts to escape.

All the clapping going on reminded me of the fireworks at a Fourth of July celebration. These cats were carrying guns and weren't afraid to let lead fly. I had no other choice but to run. It was the best thing I could do. I mean I'm gangsta and would rather be bussin' back at them but these three here walking toward me, plus the one driving the car, meant that it had to be about four of them. I held on to my nine millimeter with an empty clip and a wish.

"Yo ya'll fuckin' kill me and that's all-out war! Y'all be dead. So why don't we just put da guns down and...Y'all ain't see nuthin, nuthin till my peeps come huntin' for y'all." I yelled then sat completely out of breath watching as they drew closer and closer. I could hear the yelling and name calling accompanied by rapid gunfire. I kept out of sight thinking of what I could do against these niggas coming hard at me. I peeked before making my move while rounds were spitting at me.

"Go to fucking hell, moron'. Tell Satan we sent ya."

Guns blasted. I covered up, dodged and ducked. The voices grew thunderous. For a second all I heard was the echoing going on in my brain. It scrambled my thoughts and made it difficult for me to think.

"Yo, y'all fucking around. My crew will hunt y'all to the grave. Ya heard me?"

"Which fucking crew's gonna hunt me, puta?"

"Tell em sons-o-bitches to come get some a Carlos. I'm da man round here."

"Show that faggot no mercy. Shoot his lights out!"

Guns continued ablaze. I bounded from the trash heap after the firing ceased. I could hear their voices. I waited my turn as soon as they weren't looking my way then I'd be out. The voices came closer.

"Where's that little pussy at?"

"Come out and play little pussy..."

They were clowning me as they drew closer and closer. I heard the taunts and the whistles. I had to make my move. I did and the gunfire resumed.

"Wet that nigga up. Don't let him get away!"

Again, a burst of lead came at my head. No more time for thinking and planning just reacting. The only action was to run. I sucked up the pain, limping and dragging my leg. I knew I'd chosen this life of crime that could end any time but now I struggled to hold on to my life. Ain't gangsters supposed to die?

Their anger came through quite clear. Huffing and puffing, I was running as best I could. I felt pain beginning to tear my insides apart and I was bleeding like a stuck hog. I wanted to get away in the worse way so I limped some then hopped and ran as hard as my injured leg would allow. Pain seared through my back and thigh. I thought I'd lost them when suddenly I heard voices fuming mad.

"There he is!"

"Get him, get him don't let him escape!"

They yelled as they tried to catch me. I bobbed and wove my way through passengers standing on the platform that grimaced after seeing my blood stained clothes. Some shrieked hysterically and pointed with horrified looks on their faces as I struggled past them. Blood squirted from holes in my chest. I became woozy from the bleeding. The white wife-beater I was wearing was now crimson red.

I was determined to not let 'em catch up to me but was I really running while dead? I suddenly lost balance, tumbled while attempting to limp to the Token Booth. My bloody appearance made a tumultuous statement causing a wave of panic. The clerk saw me coming, took one good look, and I witnessed deadly fright written over her face. "It wasn't supposed to end like this," was my last thought before the frightened clerk yelled.

"Ohmigod! Somebody call the police!" She screamed. I saw her collapse then I passed out.

Minutes later, I could sense the police swarming on the scene. They attempted to take a statement but I couldn't give them one. The cold seeped in as my blood flowed freely on the concrete. I tried to focus but my eyes rolled uncontrollably as the paramedics started to work on what was left of my bloody mess.

"These gunshots look real serious," I heard one of them shout.

"We're losing him." The other began pumping hard against my chest. Weakened I could barely stay awake, but I knew I had to. My life depended on me doing so.

Seconds away from death, the paramedics took their time in carting me off on a gurney going to Kings County. Just another routine stop in this life of crime I had chosen. Some people say the situation makes the person. Going on this journey, bullet holes leaking blood from my body was par for the course. For me, I had chosen this lifestyle. This situation was unavoidable.

The siren sounded loud as the ambulance wailed miles away from the hospital. Meanwhile, I was still seconds from being another fatally sad reminder on the landscape of urban American reality.

Ma'dukes had warned me that it would end like this. I could hear her voice ringing in my head when she told me; "all mobsters eventually get locked away for life or get carried out leaving their loved ones to mourn. They never ever walk away." The ol' earth told me going down this road would be a life sentence. She had been wrong before. It's ending this way because I wanted to be gangster. No one to save me – Everyone was too busy judging me.

I could still hear that mouth of Ma'dukes. All the time she be bitching and griping about everything from welfare check to welfare check.

"You're gonna be nothing but a common thug. You can't keep robbing people everyday. Someone's gonna kill you." She was always griping about something, like her welfare money. Growing up there was always something going wrong.

"Why don't they give me more money? I can't survive on these few pennies. They know I got two chil'ren and things are expensive," Ma'dukes would whine all the time. Whenever I'd be stupid enough to agree, she'd let me have it.

"Yeah, ma I think they should give us more money," I'd say, "The government ain't trying to let us live, they want us barely surviving..."

I would never be able to finish. Ma'dukes would be refueled and ready to jump down my throat.

"Yeah, since you agree why don't you go out and get yourself a real job instead of sitting there writing nursery rhymes?"

She'd put me on full blast and ridiculed me one too many times in front of my younger sister, Lindsay. My mother never offered teaching, only criticism. Her name's Donna Parrister and she had a mouth on her that kept going loud and strong all day, annoyingly long. Without any real proof, my mother made the claim that we were descendants of Blackfoot Indians. One sunny afternoon way back, supposedly some white men captured and raped her great-great-great grandmother. That was the reason we shared the family heirloom: hazel eyes. The gene supposedly ran in a family that I never met, never knew.

We called city housing our home and lived there all our lives. No relatives ever came to visit us. I wore my inheritance well though. These hazel eyes of mine got me plenty attention from the broads. My mother always told me this:

"You just can't get anything on good looks alone," she'd say when girls started calling me on the regular at home. "Pooh, why you got these hood rats calling my phone every few minutes? I will put a lock on this phone because you're not paying any bills up in here."

"What's up, mom?" I'd ask when I could no longer ignore her.

"You wanna know what's up?" She'd start and then it would go nonstop. "You need to go out and bring in some money every now and then, that's what's up! If you ain't gonna go to school, you'd best go get yourself a job so you can have some damn money and stop depending on me. I'm not gonna be living up in here supporting your lazy ass." It would go on 'blah, blah, blah...'

I wasn't really hearing her. I'd sit there concentrating on poetry lines and tune her out until she threw criticism at my poems.

"You just sitting there at the table like some lil' bitch writing damn rhymes! Why don't you go out and do something?" Or her favorite line: "You ain't gonna 'mount to nothing." At which point she'd realize that I wasn't paying her any attention and she'd turn to my sister. "Lindsay, pass da remote, girl, and don't be like your brother. He's just another lazy ass."

That was a sure sign Ma'dukes didn't know what she was talking about. As I grew up, I proved her wrong. There was never unity in the family at home so I was destined to find one on the outside, in the streets of Brooklyn.

As the ambulance progressed through these same streets stalled by early morning traffic, I felt life slowly easing on and knew I would never live to see the sunlight again. I didn't live the street-life, I thugged it. Me and my peeps, we took it over with heart, gloves, masks and guns blazing anytime. My eyes tear as I squint uncontrollable. I'm dying alone but my peeps will be there.

In the beginning we were inseparable, always down with each other. There was Squeeze, Promise, Show, and the baby of the bunch, me, Pooh. We strangled the street-hustle with so much force that everything came in a smash. From day one, they were tight with me. Older fellows but always looked out for me. I enjoyed hanging with them and eventually we became a crew. They were all I had.

They dreamt of being filthy rich. Each wanted to control a sector of the crack industry. While they hustled, I was the lookout steering customers to my crew and telling lies to keep Jakes away.

Next stop, I was doing hand to hands for a small take until I became a full partner. We financed big drug deals with Dominicans. Takes from all that money became Mickey Mouse games to me. I wanted that big money since I was a lil' shorty in Brownsville.

Growing up poor and knowing my family could barely make it, I wanted more. It was so bad sometimes that we'd recycle gifts at Christmas. My sister and I were too young at the time to really care, but at school when classmates got mad at us, we'd get ragged-on.

"Whose turn is it to get the fruitcake in your family?"

Kids teased us at school. Life was hard but we were young and having fun living it but the guidance counselor said I had "anger issues which lead to my behavioral problems." I enjoyed myself and always liked writing poetry. After being picked on a couple times by classmates, I stopped showing my poems and stuck around until the 6th grade. I had to leave because I was getting into fights on a daily basis. But dropping out did not quench my thirst, I'd still compose poetry. It was the softer side of me that teachers and family knew but from the rest of society, I kept it hidden. I didn't want that side of me exposed 'cause where I'm from that'd make you look like cream puff. And you didn't want *soft* on your resume.

I came up rough and tough in a place where you scrambled for everything you wanted. The wild side of a Brooklyn housing section known as Roosevelt houses was a place called Do or Die that I'd made my rest. You could call it my home. Me and my peeps, Squeeze, Show, and Promise made out like bandits. We were ripping and robbing drug dealers and their clients. We figured if we could supply the supplier then we'd be the number one suppliers and set up biz along Fulton and Throop.

Some will ask why I chose the life of crime and I'll be the first to tell you. It was partly about wanting not to be broke but it was also about the love of balling and the rep. As a shorty on the come up, seeing my family as poor as could be, I didn't want that to keep happening. Being born poor is like a disease you inherit. The only way to survive it is to make a lot of money. That's why I hung with the big boys watching 'em hustle, knowing that one day I'd be on. After I learned my lessons, I started doing my thing on the streets. I learned from the jump that everything you need was here; all that money, power and respect. The ol' heads taught me that when niggas know how you got down dirty for ya cheddar, they'd give you that respect. It was that, straight up.

They told me that the road to the riches wasn't laced with sands of gold but with bullet holes and long prison terms. And once you committed, once you walked down the road, there was no turning back. The street was like a jealous lover. Out here, you couldn't love nothing but the freedom to do you because everything that you fell in love with, the streets would take right back. Whether its broads, clothes, hoes, family, friends, pussy, money, a new BM, or your latest weapon, the streets giveth and taketh. No questions asked.

The other love you have is the protection you carry inside your waistband. Whether that's a forty-five or a nine, it would enhance your chance to survive on the streets. Ol' heads' are big on respect. Respect your set or crew. And keep everything you do between you and the crew. No matter what, never become a snitch. That's signing your suicide note. On the streets, they may drink and laugh with you but in the end, nobody gives a fuck about friend. Killing you to protect their dough is just part of the way cash flows.

Me? I was always on the hunt for the next broad and then the next broad to replace my ex, constantly searching for the next broad to make her place my own. Man, if I tell you once I'll say it twice. I roamed. It was my only weakness. Whichever broad I'd catch, my head would be on her pillow to the next morn then I was out. I did the deed then on to the grind with my peeps.

My nigs and I would hang out all day long, thugging ghettonomics. At nights out on these streets, we would watch the crack fiends resurface like roaches. We'd catch them trying to get their breath and sell them more rocks cut from our freshest stock. They'd be starving for the base, hunting and makin' promises to pay like they'd have the money the next day. But we already knew there'd be no tomorrow. "Pay now," we'd say, "we don't want know brains or coochie...money talks..." That was the motto.

Getting brains for a piece of rock was a common thing. Fiends are greedy and very early we saw the potential for tremendous growth in the crack industry.

Squeeze had an idea to rob from the big timers and sell to the street hustlers for a nice price. They would peddle the drugs on the streets and be hooked to our prices. Around the hood, we supplied the suppliers. Quickly the dealers became not only customer number one but they were also targets.

After doing a day's dirt at the 'do or die', I'd creep back late nights to Brownsville where I held down a crash-pad I'd rented after moving out Ma'dukes' apartment. There, I slept sedated by the heavy sounds of my neighbors having sex. Then, like clockwork, the loud barking of gunshots would wake me. This was the late nineties. Our set riffed and tussled, handling our biz like bullies in a playpen executing our grind out on the streets of New York. I was down forever with those cats I hung with on the regular.

Promise, with his baby momma drama, he became the older brother I didn't want, always trying to steer me out of harm's way. In the beginning I looked up to him.

Squeeze, he was like the nigga all the other kids wanna be like. Every team needed one like him. He had heart. I've seen Squeeze bust this cat straight in the face for saying some dumb shit and then calling his girl ugly. Squeeze did have some ugly broads for real though, but if you ain't know him like that you couldn't say shit to him bout that. Whenever that nigga felt like he was dissed it would be all out war. I rolled with him so I should know or you could ask my other man, Show.

Show would tell you the truth 'cause he don't give a fuck. He's a big ass black ugly mutha-fucka! Matter fact, Show, big and ugly enough for three people, maybe four. It didn't matter though because he was a college bound all-star football player. Pretty broads would cling to him like static to wool. Show would have prettier broads than everyone else around except for the *kid*, of course.

So many bitches, so little time. I can't even begin to name them all. I remember when it all started. See, I was blessed with the fucking cute hazel eyes that made bitches go wild. I'd hit a blunt or smoke some o' bomb-bomb zee with a bitch and my eyes would get to changing colors, ooh-wee. Lovemaking would be off the hinges.

Whenever I stared in a broad's eyes, I could see them fantasizing about wanting to fuck me. All I had to do was snap my fingers and panties would drop. Bitches love a handsome thug and that's what I was. They would glance at me and if they looked more than once, it was over. I'd be at a party and get tapped on the shoulder and it would be the dopest broad just waiting to dance with me.

"Hi, I don't know if you've noticed that I've been waiting here for you to dance wit' me."

It would be the prettiest something in the spot and she'd be on me like that. My niggas would stay mad cause I'd just steady take their little girlfriends. Bring your girl around me and if she looked in my eyes, it was on.

Every night since I was about thirteen, if I wasn't hustling I'd be beating up some cunt. I was blessed, ya heard! Yeah, the good girls, I can still see them even now creaming, watching my eyes going from fiery red to green. The colors would go from green to brown to blue to purple or anything a broad wanted to see. Just stare into my hazel eyes and that fire would start down below the navel. Girls, they love that kinda shit. Legs be trembling and pussy be wet... I'm getting ahead of myself.

The gang of us would meet over at Squeeze's pad or in the basement where his uncle stayed. Squeeze would kick his spiel then we'd all break out and later that evening, hit niggas up. We'd hit them up and break out as usual. It was a really simple job. No need for sweating. Squeeze liked to go sell that shit for bargain prices to some people he knew out in South Jersey. Me, I preferred going further down south to places like B'More and all that dark country metro area, down south to D-ware and all them parts.

I remember once we'd gotten about thirty pounds off these cats out in Philly and then we called Squeeze's peeps out in B'More. They couldn't pay cash for it so they told us about their man in Virginia who could sponsor the weight. We spoke to him on the phone and he invited us down to VA.

I remembered we met Harry at some upscale club. He was a fool and thought that because we partied with him and his girls, we wouldn't rob him. Maybe it was the baby blue Cadillac we rolled up in.

That weekend was Show's birthday. He bought the ride and had it tricked out. Harry made several offers for the whip. He liked our style and the way we handled our BI. We were rocking crushed linen Armani suits. It was either the champagne or maybe the way we conducted ourselves.

Something we did put Harry's head in a spin. The risk had already been calculated. We were only gonna bag his dumb ass for some big cash. Except in the process, I also caught my first body.

We met him while mobbing up in the club. Harry was a big man, tan with a mid-east accent and a love for Moet. Like gentlemen, it was Show's birthday weekend and we splurged a little. Squeeze was always running his mouth about biz, talking loudly and getting us all kinds of attention, some unwanted but mostly wanted. Harry, who claimed he was the man, sat at our table and enjoyed our celebration. We quickly learned all about his stable of mules. They were running on Peter Pans back and forth, north to south, east to west. His girls were charming and they doubled as his only security.

"What crazy fool would wanna hurt any of these beautiful women?" Harry threw out as he spoke glowingly of his stable.

He traveled light except for his girls. He hated violence. There was no security except for these six broads. Man that just didn't make sense when you were in the type of biz we were in. The more we found out about Harry, the more we knew he was the next victim. I listened to the chatter then got bored when the conversation turned into another *Squeeze sting*. He would make crazy claims of what we were holding, mostly lies. Then the *mark* would boast of what they've got. Eventually Squeeze would decide if the cat was fat enough for us to bag. I liked Harry's girls and danced off with two. Later, Squeeze met us at the bar.

"Excuse me ladies, bizness before pleasure," I said and dismissed the two broads. Promise and Show joined us.

"Besides Harry loving all that Mo, what else did you find out about Harry?"

"Yeah, that nigga do drink a lot of champagne, dogs," Squeeze said with a smile.

"Word up. When you left, we ordered like four more bottles and half went down his fucking throat."

"He claimed that around here they call him the H-Man and he be sitting on stacks of cheddar."

"Let's fuck his bitches," Show said. "That'll be a good weekend."

"Nah, we could do that later son," Squeeze started. "This mutha-fucka wants us to go back to the *telly* with him and guess what?"

"What, what?" Show shouted as if he was holding the winning ticket in a lottery drawing. We all looked at him. Squeeze continued to talk about robbing this fool and I focused on bagging a couple of his broads.

Harry's mules were scheduled to arrive about three thirty in the morning. They were coming from the bus depot. This nigga was so impressed with our sale that he was trying to get us to buy some keys off him. He thought we were the *legit* bizness type. In a way we were but we really weren't. We sold the fool twenty pounds of quality 'dro we'd lifted off some other fools in Newark at gunpoint.

Normally, that grade of weed could run you anywhere from three to four grand a pound. Since he was buying it all and paying cash on delivery, we gave him all twenty for fifty grand. Real bargain for us considering we ain't spent nothing but gas and tolls. We knew the weed was good enough and I don't know what Squeeze told him about us. This cat was so impressed by our way of doing business that he wanted us to see just how major his operation really was. About three in the morning, we left the club and rode a few miles to the Day's Inn. Harry had a couple adjoining rooms. Music and champagne flowed freely. We had to wait around to collect our fifty grand anyway.

Harry enjoyed DMX. The music blasted as we partied up with his six girls. Squeeze, Show, and I all had our manhood's *glazed* by these broads. Even though we were celebrating Show's birthday, Promise was fronting like he wasn't feeling too good. Time passed and we were getting edgy waiting for the dough so we could bounce. It was getting closer to that time when the mules would come. We were carefully monitoring H-Man when he approached us with another offer.

"Listen guys, down here in VA things do move slower than up north where y'all from. Because it's taking longer than I expected to get all of the cash and I know you've been patient with me, I've got a deal. How you say it? I've got a fat ass deal for you."

"Okay, okay," Squeeze said and all our ears perked.

"I've got a major shipment coming through. Y'all could stick around and take some back up to Boston with you," Harry said with a smile.

Promise looked shook and started giving off worried signals with his face but Harry continued, "You gave me a very nice price on that smoke. I'd surely like to return the favor." He was wearing a smile that was either deceiving or devious. "It's taking too long to come up with that fifty thousand so here's what I'm thinking of doing. I'll give you twenty five thousand cash and your other half in some good white powder," he said to our surprise.

We were thinking Harry was coming to us with short money or telling us to wait another day. This fool was offering us both drugs and money. Now to four thugs outta Brooklyn, that was a damn good offer. How could we turn it down? Now we had to rob Harry the pimp of his drugs and cash. How could one man be so trusting?

"We gotta discuss this amongst us," Promise said still acting a little petro.

After sitting down next to a mini bar, Promise said nothing but winked to the camera. This could be a set up. Maybe Harry's plan was not to let us leave the 'State for Lovers' with his money. We knew what had to be done and shook our heads. Finally, Squeeze whispered below his breath, "Let's take the money and drugs, dogs."

"I got a bad feeling..." Promise stated, but Squeeze had already decided. It was his call and for the first time I saw a tinge of yellow seeping from the mouth of Promise.

"Let's do the deal," Squeeze said. He looked around in each of our eyes. "There are a lot of ways we could do this but if the coke is good, let's take it."

"Are you saying what I thinking you're saying, Squeeze?" Show asked. He was so slow.

"Yeah nigga! Something wrong with your brain?" Squeeze answered immediately.

"I mean, we could get that and take that back and make some more money on top of it," I said.

"We can't be dealin' coke in certain hoods, you know?" Show said raising his hand in doubt.

"Fuck that! Ain't nobody telling me where I can or cannot hustle in my hood, dogs," Squeeze said getting testy.

"Aiight, so we wit' it then."

Everyone laid hands like we were a varsity team ready to execute the next big play. It was like that, the dirty game we were playing where our guns made us most viable players. We partied until the doorbell rang and these three fine broads strolled in. It was time for the fun to really begin.

They appeared to be your average sexy looking broads with the bodies of dancers. One look and you could immediately tell that they were carrying heavy weights. Once we identified who *we* were, all we had to do was get into position. They were very beautiful broads and we'd already scripted the play. Looking at all these beautiful women around the room made me think that this Harry fellow was probably pimping. I hoped we had no problems cause I'd hate to catch a body. I would if any of these broads try something crazy, I kept thinking the whole time.

So now the hotel room was abuzz with activity. Six scantily clothed broads wearing only bras and panties were sprawled on a huge bed, chillin'. One other broad was there somewhere. Our attention turned to the two mules in the other room with Harry. We had discussed the situation as a "just in case" way to escape. Promise had volunteered to get the car. He was about to make his move when Harry walked back into the room smiling.

"Here is your twenty five thousand dollars," he said moving slowly. I walked to the bathroom as planned and opened the door. It was a routine robbery except we knew we were being recorded and that meant we couldn't leave without the video. I sat on the stool and took the weapon off safety. Careful not to drop the gun in the toilet bowl, I slipped the silencer on it. I began to walk out then turned back and flush the toilet. As soon as I opened the door, I was to blast him if Harry did anything sudden. The door pushed opened and I held the nine on them waiting to do exactly that. Everyone standing either ducked or was running and screaming. In that chaos, Squeeze, whose eyes had been following the drugs, made his move through the door.

"What the fuck are you doing? You're gonna have the cops all over this place in seconds," Harry shouted.

I kept the gun on him while we waited until Squeeze came out with the coke. My hand sweated a little when Squeeze took too long. My palm gripped the nine tighter. I pulled the twenty-two out of my boot just in case. Meantime, Promise had ducked out and rushed downstairs to the parking lot. His bitch-ass didn't wanna be in the line of fire so he went to secure the car. I was thinking that nigga wanted to live to care for his daughter, ducking out when things start popping off. Not me, I was built for this. I waited several gut wrenching minutes. It seemed like half hour but I had to make sure my nigga Squeeze was alright.

All the time, Harry was cursing and screaming, "I thought you guys were businessmen. You're no businessmen. You're common thugs."

I yoked Harry and walked him to the bedroom door. He opened it and we saw Squeeze with his face up in the broad's ass looking like he was eating her out.

"Ah mutha-fucka, you got to get your fucking sex on at this moment?" Show asked.

"Nigga, I'm trying to get all the coke outta this bitch!" Squeeze said turning around for a couple of seconds then back to the task at hand, removing the coke from the broad's coochie.

"We can work all this out. I've got millions…"

"Shush, Harry, you just tell me where the video is and I'll let your punk ass live," I said and he pointed to the camera. Show popped his middle finger at it and grabbed the camera. In a flash, we'd be out. As we walked out the room, Harry was still pleading with Squeeze about the big error he'd made.

"You guys can still profit from this business. We don't have to rip each other off. I'm a good man, I understand. I'll forgive y'all for this."

"Really, we don't need your forgiveness," Squeeze said and that's was when one of the mules fired a shot from behind.

I turned to see Harry fall then I saw the mule holding the smoking forty-five in her hand. I was seconds away from filling this crazed broad with holes but I noticed she only fired once hitting Harry in his back. He never knew who plugged him.

"Y'all mutha-fuckin' New York niggas ain't leaving with all the profits," she said aiming the gun side to side trying to cover all of us. We hadn't calculated this bit. I was ready to break this broad off some lead when Squeeze spoke up.

"Aiight, so what you gonna do. Shoot all of us?"

"I ain't saying I wanna kill any of y'all. It's that bitch ass Harry I couldn't stand. I wanna make a deal."

"What you talking 'bout?" Show asked.

"I figured we took a lot of risk and we ain't getting a penny so I'm thinking y'all niggas could hit me with some dough and we'll be straight." She was still holding the forty-five. I could have blasted her but Squeeze got mushy on me.

"I respect your gangsta but I can't give you what ain't mine, shorty," he said.

"I got kids to feed. This drug money was gonna go a long way, you could split some of your share," she proposed.

"You trying to rob me, bitch?" Squeezed asked as his cell phone rang. I had a feeling that it was Promise. He was probably wondering what was keeping us here so long.

Squeeze handed the phone to Show. I was right, it was Promise. Show turned away under the watchful glance of the freak with a gun in her hand.

"This bitch up here tryin…" he started then the broad started getting other ideas. Maybe she thought we were sweet in our Armani suits, sipping champagne and carrying guns because we wannabes. But she opened her mouth and I knew shit was fixing to get all out nasty. I knew somebody was gonna die and it wasn't gonna be from my side.

"Put the phone down!" She yelled and my finger that had been itching for the longest minute seemed to just react and the gun blasted the broad back down. She fell like a sack of bloody mess while the other broads who were crouching everywhere squealed loudly.

"We out, dogs," Squeeze said as another broad fired a shot barely missing me.

"Eat lead, bitch," I yelled as the nine went off in my hand. Her body jerked hard. She sprawled on top of the desk. I turned and pointed the nine at the others. They sucked in their breath and fell silent.

We rushed out the door leaving the carnage. Harry was laid out making the carpet red and the two broads were bloody in another room. The other scantily clad broads were trying to get their clothes on as I slammed the door and raced downstairs to the parking lot.

"Let's be out. Let's move, dogs," Squeeze shouted. We hopped into the car and tires peeled heading to 95 North.

"What the fuck was the problem wit' y'all niggas? Y'all taking y'all sweet old time fucking around wit' them bitches, while I'm down here trying to figure what the fuck done happened!" Promise said sounding like he was shook. He looked at Squeeze who'd sat up front, then he looked at me and Show in the back through the rearview. No one answered until Show pulled out all the money and coke along with some of the weed we'd sold earlier to Harry.

"We had a small problem," I stated.

"Word? I was down here worried. I thought y'all was up there having an orgy wit' them bitches and that…" Promise started to speak but was cut off by Squeeze.

"Them bitches? They played themselves, dog," Squeeze said.

Promise took his eyes off the road for couple seconds and turned around to glance at all the money and drugs. A frown appeared on his face when he recognized blood on the money.

"Yo, y'all had to shoot some…" he began to say but I jumped in.

"Yeah nigga! I had to shoot them two bitches. They pulled out guns dog, and blam!" I said with my fingers shooting air.

Squeeze and I chuckled when Show fell against the car seat as if he'd caught a bad one. I began to laugh but Promise didn't want to see the humor.

"Blam, blam," Show shouted then mocking the broads with a high-pitched tone he started, "Oh, you shot me, fool. You shot me. I was jest tryin' to rob you."

Show was only living up to his name. He used to be a high school football player who would dance from the knowledge of ruining some quarterback's career with a devastating hit. Now he was laughing at the way those broads died. I guess his impulse was to make light of bad situations.

Promise was just not feeling us. He screamed at me.

"You young ass fucking crazy fool, you knew the nigga had a camera! Your gun's gonna get us all put away. I'm a tell y'all right here, I ain't living in no jail, dogs."

"*Stop worrying so much*!" I said to him then looked at Show and asked, "You got the tape right, Show?"

Everyone but Promise knew that Show had the videotape. I wanted to see the reaction from Promise once he found out that the tape was secured. I knew that that he was gonna still be bitching up.

"See nigga. Now you ain't gotta worry 'bout shit else, aiight," Show said and stripped the film from the tape. "Here, Promise you can hold this. We even got you a camera too." He laughed. Promise glanced at him with a scowl on his face.

"Ha, ha very funny, huh Show? It don't matter. I'm saying y'all going the fuck overboard." Promise looked around for support but we all knew it was either the broads or us. "Going from state to state collecting these bodies' gonna make us too fucking hot," he said.

"Too fucking hot is what we want nigga," I said.

"Oh word, that's what you want huh?" Promise asked

"I'm saying dogs, we family and if I see someone raise a gun, I have no choice but to shoot to kill 'cause that's fam'," I said.

"Yeah nigga, them bitches was trying to blast me and Show. The bitch done shot her pimp and then she was fixing to rob us. You feel me?" Squeeze asked and handed me a pound. "That gave Pooh no choice, she had to die."

"All I'm saying is; we've got to slow down with the gun play."

"I'm saying nigga; I'm the one taking the burden. That was my finger on the trigger of my fucking gun spraying them bitches. Why is yo ass acting so petro? You ain't done shit and I ain't gonna ask *you* to hold the weight."

"That's real right there," Show said and kept dumping the bag of the bounty in the space between me and him in the back seat of the caddy. Four nice size bags of coke, about a kilo, fell on the redone suede leather of the car.

We were still strapped with the twenty pounds of weed and about thirty five thousand dollars in cash. Pulling through a McDonald's drive-thru allowed us time to ponder the possibilities over some cheeseburgers, cokes and fries.

As we sat around in the parking lot rest stop, Show grabbed a bag of the white powdery stuff and examined it carefully before putting some to his lips. Then he licked it off with his tongue. He swirled it around like an expert wine taster.

"Shit's the real fucking thing, man! This some pure shit too, dogs," Show said and continued dipping and sniffing. "Hmm…not bad, not bad, this real cocaine," he said with another whiff. He stuffed his nostrils with white powder. His face flushed. Show was having a happy birthday weekend. That nigga was now getting older.

"Happy birthday, big Show," I said and sniffed a little of the coke. We laughed because he was right. This was some good cocaine. We could tap dance on this and still come off huge. Wanting in on the action, Squeeze turned around looking amped.

"Yeah, what you think about that, huh, niggas?" We glad-handed and Squeezed rolled somethin'.

You could tell Squeeze was hyped, he couldn't contain himself. Promise on the other hand he seemed too withdrawn and was even trying to bright side. "I'm aiight, I'm aiight," he would say between bites of his meal but through the strain, we all could tell he was keeping something hidden deep inside.

I couldn't see his heart but his face told the story. For some reason, try as he might; Promise just wasn't himself at all. He stared straight ahead and remained tight-lipped all the way. The only person who sat up front cheesing was Squeeze. Promise seemed like he wanted no part of us.

"Aw shit!" Show exclaimed, "This da best fucking birthday a nigga ever had. Y'all my dogs. Yo, Promise don't be scared to pump the volume on my shit, nigga," he yelled and clapped his hands when the music serenaded him.

Squeeze got on the phone and in a few minutes, was on the line with a major player up in Greenwich. He agreed to get some of the cocaine off our hands. We gave him a good price as he would send the courier before the end of the day with cash. Things were bubbling.

Although dumping the drugs was gonna be an easy thing, there was a rapid decline in everyone's motivation. Out of the haul we would only keep a few onions for the niggas to steam when we were chilling, nothing more. None of us in the clique were real drug heads. We were recreational users and businessmen.

After we got back to BK from the VA. trip, I could see the changes taking place in that nigga, Promise.

On the days we'd hustle, he was coming through less and less. Squeeze would come up with ideas and dough-making schemes that had made us who we were, hustlers above all other sets. Over a short period of time on this Brooklyn landscape we earned the label, Notorious, like Biggie Smalls.

Yet we slowed down a lot. There was time for about a week where the four of us were not together. This hadn't happen in awhile but ever since the VA thing, niggas seemed like they were falling back. I had thought this was what we wanted, all this dough from our gangster-ism. One day as we sat in the basement, in between tokes of a blunt, I voiced my opinion.

"Y'all niggas acting like y'all just don't know. Once you got the streets watching, you got to live up to that 'cause niggas gonna see you slippin'."

"Who say we slippin'?"

"Hold up man, let me explain what I'm talkin' about, nigga. I'm saying word on the streets is that we're slippin. You know things get sheisty when niggas start thinking that way. Mugs be thinking it's the best time to come at a nigga. Yo, I be out there grindin'. I know what's up."

"Yeah? That's what's being kicked around out there? That's what you hear? All I got to say is; me personally, I ain't slippin'. Niggas imagine that and I'll lay a mutha-fucka out. You feel me?" Show was getting up and waving his tool around.

Squeeze watched him and then said, "Yo Show be careful you don't fuck up my television, aiight."

"Pass the dro, nigga," Promise said. He inhaled heavy and blew a cloud smoke on the rest of us.

"Easy nigga, you stressed?" Squeeze asked but Promise didn't answer and kept puffing.

"Niggas step to me and I'm not gonna hesitate to smack a nigga down. I don't care; I'll catch a case..." Show was saying when I cut him off.

"Man, stop talking all that going to jail shit."

"I'm saying, dogs. I'll blow a nigga away like you blew them bitches away down in VA. With this automatic shit, I'll what…niggas betta not run up to me looking tough."

"Show, stop kicking all that bullshit... Uncle Junior? Where that nigga at? Uncle Junior!" Squeezed yelled until finally his uncle walked quickly in the living room. "What you doing back there? I hope you ain't smoking up any coke back there, Uncle Junior. I swear if I find that you stealing any coke from back there…"

"Why you call me to come at me like that? I was in the toilet."

"In the toilet doing what?"

"Taking care of my biz. What do you want Squeeze?"

"Let me find out that you smoking any coke in my damn bathroom. I swear they gonna have to surgically remove these Tims from up outta your mutha fuckin' asshole."

"You wanna throw out threats, nigga?"

"Aiight, I'm just sayin. Yo twist up about four blunts."

Promise raised his hand, choking for a few minutes. "I'm good, dogs."

"That just means more blunts for us niggas," Squeeze said with his wry smile. "Gotcha you on that, my nigga," he said pointing at Promise. They both laughed and anyone could sense the camaraderie but at a closer glance, there was evidence of strain on Promise's face.

"It ain't about killing anyone, it's about making that money, man," Squeeze said and gave his uncle the weed he needed to roll. He also gave him five dollars.

"Go to the store and bring me back a pack of Dutchmasters."

"Oh, so that was the reason for you hollerin' out my name."

"Just go on and hurry back, man! I ain't got time for your ol' ass. I got bizness to handle right now, you feel me?" Squeeze dismissed his uncle. He waited till he had walked out the room before continuing.

"Look, when all this 'yes' shit stops, niggas will be surprised when we hit them. It's all good to fall back and regroup. Ain't none of us starving," Promise said but he was not convincing anyone. We knew each other from when we were kids. There was something that was being left unsaid.

"Yo, I gotta say that I agree. It is about the money but we gotta wait for niggas to fuck up, then we hit them," Squeeze said.

"Yeah but the last time we did anything was about three weeks ago," I stated.

"That's good nigga. We got fat while a lot of other mutha-fuckas starved. Let 'em have their run. Maybe we should fall back for a hot minute and..." Promise said and I immediately interrupted.

"Why? When we come back out, niggas ain't gonna respect us like they did..."

"Come on man, you bullshitting, Pooh. See you too young to understand that everything takes time...you got dough, a nice car and..." Show started but I was too hot to listen.

"Man, I want more. This shit we talking 'bout right here, that's chump change for other niggas right next door to us."

"You can't be comparing yourself to another nigga..." Promise began saying.

Our voices trailed off when the door opened and Uncle Junior walked in. He scurried pass us to the kitchen.

"Go roll that inside the bedroom, Uncle Junior," Squeeze ordered.

"First, I had to go the store then you're gonna tell me where I should go to roll your weed? C'mon get real!"

"If you don't get your bitch-ass da fuck outta here right now, I'm gonna..."

"Keep your shirt on, nigga. I'll go to the bedroom and roll," Uncle Junior said and carefully scraped up all the weed and walked out. "Yeah I better go. Y'all look very heated. Who done boned whose girl? What's done is done," Uncle Junior said in passing.

"Get da fuck out Uncle! Ain't nobody got time for your tired bitch ass questions," Squeeze said. We waited for Uncle Junior to rush out before continuing.

"Yo y'all know we holding down a lil' bit of cheddar. So it's all good for us to fall back a little somethin'."

"Yeah but the other side about that is the streets see all 'laying low' as weakness."

"Listen young un, I agree wit' these niggas," Show said and pointed to Promise and Squeeze.

"We know what we holding, but if we fall back the streets might just take that for weakness and we wind up being victims..." I began to say but Squeeze raised his hand and started speaking.

"Right now I ain't saying a crew can't come at us but we gotta be real. It ain't like before dog, we got shit to lose," Squeeze said and waved his hand around. Uncle Junior walked in with four blunts. "Good looking out, Uncle. Them shits rolled like you hanging wit' the dreadlock brothas on Fulton." Squeeze laughed and quickly sparked one.

He threw out a blunt one to each of us like when we were shorties and robbed the candy stores in the hood. We had been through a lot but this was like a breaking up. All we need is niggas to start singing 'Kum-by-ya'. Squeeze offered a light. Promise took the blunt but he never lit his. I grew up admiring that nigga. Now he had gone from hard to cream puff and it wasn't a good look. But I know it all had to do with the love for his daughter. So I guess I couldn't really fault the nigga.

I puffed the blunt thinking that our gangster clique was about to break down. As further proof these niggas had gotten comfortable like the older niggas we had seen growing up, the conversation quickly change to a discussion about broads.

"Yo, there's a bitch in 2A, I saw that bitch in the club last week Friday..."

"Yeah, she's got a dope body. What's her name?"

"Yo, Promise, I know that honey got some friends, hook a nigga up..."

We all puffed knowing that there was no way back. Promise and Squeeze wanted to fall back. Fuck that! We had to keep this going. We had that saying, "We number one." How we gonna fall back? It's like if a bully stopped fighting, the lack of action could give other weaker ones the heart to come at you. Then it'll be gunning in the streets.

"Lets move out of state, set up something new. VA..." I started to suggest but was quickly chopped down.

"Nah, I'm thinking we lay low. I mean if sure money comes this way then we work that. Promise is right. We could still live well. Do something in a couple of months..." Squeezed started to say before Show threw his two-cents in.

"Man, I got a baby on the way..." he said with the big grin.

"My daughter is important, everyone knows that for sure. I'll be the first to let y'all know that I'll be damn if I ever fuck her life up," Promise said as he stood and looked directly at me. "I gotta give her a chance, my niggas. I ain't trying to diss no one, but I'm just sayin', I can't keep acting like I only got one option..." he continued looking my way. I was furious.

"Yo, y'all are acting like bitches! Straight up! I ain't never know there'd come a day when I'd say that. That's my word, the way y'all acting right now I don't know? All I'm sayin' is yo, I'd check if y'all wearing skirts..."

"Man, fuck you!" Show screamed. He jumped and I eased my waist band exposing the nine millimeter. Show yielded to caution. "What you gonna shoot me like you did that bitch in VA., Pooh? Well you better not miss cuz..."

"That's what y'all wanna do, fight? Pull your gun out? Young un, I'm talking to you!" Squeeze said, looking dead in my grill.

"Wha' what? I just ain't gonna let a mutha-fucka intimidate my ass. I'm gonna shoot his ass if I have to," I said and realized that I really would. These niggas I started out with were growing into some big pussies.

"I ain't trying to get locked up shot up or ruin my daughter's life," Promise said. "If I run out of options then that would be different, but I'm just sayin'..."

As I puffed hard on the blunt, I said, "I ain't got no where else to go. This it for me. No turning back."

Squeeze left the room and returned a few moments later carrying enough bottles of Moet to go around. It felt like a final date or something.

We drank and toasted, hugged and laughed at each other's most ridiculous moments. Like Show drinking from one bottle and we were using another as an ashtray. Since both bottles were dark, the nigga got so drunk that without warning, he picked up the bottle being used as the ashtray and drank every single roach in it. We died laughing. We hugged and everyone was liberated with the weed and the alcohol.

It never dawned on us that this maybe was the last time we'd all sit and let loose. It was the turning point in our lives, the beginning of the end of us. The kids who started it all were no longer motivated. For whatever reason, we all had gotten too old to continue. I guess I wanted more. I was lost in my thoughts when I heard the conversation that Promise was kicking.

"…I ain't trying to get no larger in this. Right now life's good but there's more to living than this…I don't wanna have to kill anyone." I half listened.

"But them things bound to happen when you taking over," I said but Promise had made up his mind.

"Yeah but killings' gonna lead to more killings. I don't wanna be running around killing niggas, scared the police gonna shoot me or niggas gonna kill my daughter."

The words sounded foreign in the room filled with thugs. Everyone including Squeeze quaked from the boots on his feet to the air he breathed. None of us thought Promise would ever bring it up. The room went silent. Even the loud sound of the TV seemed to go suddenly mute.

Nobody had to utter a word. Promise was sounding like he was saying goodbye to the streets and to us, the clique, his buddies down like south for whatever. The whole time I was thinking of my mother and my sister, Lindsay.

I used to hear my mother nag the fuck out of her lovers. Over the years, I saw that nagging only lead to one thing. It always preceded break-up. Just before the nigga walked out on mommy, the tone would be set by her cooking a great dinner and then they would moan loudly, not caring if me or Lindsay heard them.

The morning after that final big argument, she would know it. She would hope that he would call or come back. No matter how pretty you are, no one wants to return home from a hard day to constant nagging. The important thing was what would happen the night before, the last date.

So it was that no matter how hard we tried, we all knew that this was the end. "Let's get that money, man" had been the chant motivating us. Now they had become too fat and just wanted to sit around taking care of their other responsibilities. I had given up everything to be down with them. Was I a herb, the loser, the sucker?

Sitting here drinking and puffing feeling like this was the last time we'd see each other I wanted to tell them what they meant to me. I never did. The whole situation reminded of how I delayed in telling my mother what I felt until too late. Until it had eaten away at my independence then the streets happened and I no longer cared.

'Juicy' by the Notorious BIG thumped loud and we all could relate. Maybe it was the champagne or the weed but my mind fell into reminiscing mode. I sat down with my head spinning, drifting like a log wood in an ocean of thoughts as them niggas moved on with the talk of broads.

"...I'd be fucking the bitch and the bitch so loud, she wakes up her mother and she joined us in the bed. I was bangin' both..."

The celebration was a loud, boastful goodbye to our clique. It reminded me of when we committed to making real cheddar.

The year 2000 was a grand hustle time, everyone flossed with a gun and I had two. That was for just in case. I knew being gangster took heart and I wanted to show these niggas out here that I was no joke.

On the streets, one slip and cops or niggas be salivating, waiting to bag you. I put the .22 in my Timberland boots and the 9 millie in my waistband. Fuck the jackers and the cops. I'm prepared to go to war and die if niggas fuck with family, my money or my crew.

All the meetings would be on the Ave over at Squeeze's rest. That nigga had a huge fucking crib and he had the 70" Plasma joint. We had come a long way from babies wrestling in the park to straight up mobbing.

It was lovely back then, plenty of sunshine and pretty ladies going by. Some on their way to work, others seemed in a rush to get to nowhere. One morning, I spotted one as I drove slowly in my silver 745. I crept and watched as she swished her hips from side to side. She knew I was watching so she brushed her long, light-brown, wavy hair on her slightly exposed shoulders. About five foot six, I was all over that. One thing was clear, she wasn't a hood rat. I saw the look in her dark Spanish eyes and I knew what she wanted. She wanted a man that was romantic.

Up ahead, I knew there was florist on Atlantic Ave. I pulled up to the curb, hopped out the Beamer and ran into the flower store. The place was crowded, the only clerks were too busy trimming and wrapping flowers at the counter. I waited then saw the perfect bunch of white and yellow roses inside the display door. The sign read $70 per dozen. I glanced quickly over my shoulders at the busy clerks. They were still too busy to even see me grab the flowers and run back to the Beamer.

She was walking so sexily on her way down the block that I could feel my dick starting to rise. Bouncing hips built for sexing. With pleasure I watched her then got in the car and drove away. Tracking her through my rearview, it was clear she looked good enough for me to go all the way. Everything was in place; her hair, a little tan to go with that caramel tone made her complexion perfect and she had a gorgeous face set off by some luscious lips. This broad was a dime. And you know I drove slowly peeking at that ass because it was what had first caught my attention.

Her bootie rolled around while her shapely legs vigorously strolled into my life. It was one of them exciting asses that easily bounced around with no visible effort. Love to fuck that, I thought as the plan was hatched. I was convinced that she wouldn't be able to resist this game I was about to spit.

I drove further up the block and pulled over and popped my collar. There I waited leaning against the whip, stunting with a bunch of flowers in my hand. The way my jewels shone, you could tell that this wasn't 'How to be a Player 101. From the 20 inch shoes on the BMW to the $10,000 piece on my neck I was a lover indeed, a baller with no stress.

I looked at the iced out Roly, frosty on my wrist. It was 8:30. That meant that I'd have time to get my game on and make it to Squeeze's crib. Recently, since he had to care for his seed, Promise had fallen into the habit of being late in the mornings. He had mad love for his seed and that nigga had to go through that morning routine with her. It was the type of situation that makes a nigga go soft. You know, lose heart, and start to think of getting out of the game cuz of responsibilities. That kinda shit gotta make a hard nigga mush but it doesn't really matter, he was Promise. So I knew I definitely wouldn't be the last to arrive.

Squeeze, he'll always be there on time, loud as ever be and ready for whatever. Him and his crack-head-for-a uncle, they be getting on the nerves with all that arguing in the morning. I know for sure that that nigga Show would be late any fucking how.

Show had bad bed tendencies. He be wanting to lay around watching Jerry Springer with his baby momma all day long. That nigga was the white man's best friend. His lazy ass will still be sleeping when the revolution goes down. Nigga lived a block away from Squeeze and was never on time.

Me, I wanted this gorgeous ass broad coming my way and I licked my lips 'cause I knew I had the time to pitch my game. I saw that smile slowly sneak out as she approached. Her body language said she was impressed.

"Hey good morning, Senorita how are you doing?" I said as she approached.

She said nothing at first but I saw her glance at the BMW and the shoes it sat on. She smiled when she saw the bling on my wrist and pinkie. Chicken-head, I thought as I offered her the bunch of flowers.

"Nice car," she said in a matter-of-fact tone, not even taking the flowers.

"What's your name, beautiful?"

"Natasha and yours?"

"They call me Pooh, baby. Need a lift to work?"

"No, I'm good, Pooh," she said and I couldn't tell if she was joking or not. The broad was playing me.

"What about the flowers?" I asked and the broad gave me a blasé look.

"What are those for?" She asked with an attitude that stank, but she still reached and took them. That was when I took a peek down her dress to look at her breasts and I noticed her shine. I checked the rest of her gear. She had a Fendi bag and smelled really nice so I ignored all of the warning signs and kicked it.

"They're flowers for a beautiful senorita, ma. Your perfume is very enchanting. What is it called?" I asked with a smile that couldn't be ignored.

"My-man, will you mind your damn bizness," she replied.

I couldn't believe what I was hearing. Was it that my game was just flat? "Huh uh?" that was the only response I could mutter. This broad had mad fucking attitude, I thought. She was carrying a bag with Burger King and coffee. A working girl, she had a little job and big attitude.

"Ma," I started with my plea staring into her eyes. "I want you to know that I've been dreaming about something as fine as you coming into my life. And tell me this is true so I can go and get the biggest ice from Jake's."

"Save all that. Can't you see that you've got to come with something a little better than that, homeboy."

I was undaunted for this broad was good looking and as fine as they come. The question popped into my head; was she worth the trouble? They all come running eventually. These women you meet on the streets, they all have a breaking point. I kept searching, wanting to find hers.

"You're right. I know a girl as beautiful as you probably get these proposals all day long. So give me your number and I'll give you a call and you and me can discuss this later over some dinner at the Four Seasons. Maybe we could catch a late flick and spend the night in the Penthouse suite at the Trump International. I could do all that, Ma."

"I'm not some hoochie who's gonna fall for all that bullshit," she said and looked at her watch. It was filled with stones and so too was the bracelet on her wrist. I had no choice but to use my gun.

"Ma, I want you to take off all your jewelry and give them to me!"

"Uh?" She said stunned. It was her time to be speechless, I thought as I brought the weapon closer to her ample chest. I think I saw her nipples rise and stick out like headlights. She didn't budge.

"Bitch, now you playing deaf?" I asked. "Take off all ya fucking jewelry and pass them to me. Right now, bitch," I yelled, scaring her. She did just that.

There at the street corner, on a beautiful day, I relieved this stuck-up-ass-bitch-with-attitude of all her jewels and took her Fendi bag. I emptied the bag onto the passenger side of the car and returned the empty bag to her. She had that shock look of disbelief all over her face.

"Need a ride to work bitch?" I asked as if we were friends going on our separate ways for the day. She shook her head and stood rooted to the spot.

"Aiight, then you just go ahead and have a lovely day," I said and jumped into the car.

Tires screeched and I was out. I left her standing there still frozen in her shocked state.

"Bi-yotch!" I yelled and tore up the road on my way to Squeeze's block. I pulled up and jumped out with breakfast and flowers. Just outside the building was a bus stop. An elderly lady stood patiently waiting for the next bus. I offered the bunch of flowers to her.

She took them smiled and said, "God bless you, young man. How did you know it was my birthday?"

"Something just told me," I said and walked to the building.

I rang the bell three times. Squeeze's *crack head* Uncle Junior let me into the apartment. I gave him some daps and continued to look at all the credit cards lifted earlier from the most beautiful girl in the world.

"What da fuck's a damn W4?" I asked Squeeze.

"Yo whassup wit' your man, Promise, son? I swear that nigga gonna be late for his own mutha-fuckin' funeral, son," Squeeze said, ignoring my question.

"That nigga be having executive hours, son. Talking 'bout his daughter had to go to mutha-fuckin' preschool," Show said walking from the bathroom. "Let me get one of them sausage biscuits, Pooh." I was surprise that Show was there. He was early for once.

"Easy man, I'm fucking starving nigga. That broad kept me up all fucking night. Had to put that broad to bed. Wake up and she still got my dick in her mouth, ready," I said. "I need my energy, dogs."

"Yeah, what you need to do is give a nigga a sausage biscuit and I'll hook you up wit some mo'fucking tiger bone."

"Man, what da fuck is a tiger bone?"

"Let me tell you sun, you really don't wanna fuck with that shit. I fucked ugly ass Sarah on the beach at Coney Island off that shit, son."

There was a major pause in the room. All three of us looked at each other blankly.

"You fucked ugly ass Sarah?" I asked finally.

"Yeah, son, that Tiger Bone...."

"Don't be blaming that shit on no Tiger bone, dogs. That's straight…"

"Ah, see, you don't know nothing 'bout that. That's some shit for you," Show, all muscles and no brains, said laughing.

"You don't wanna fuck with that, young un. Your young ass done kill a bitch with that shit inside of you," Squeeze said and began laying out some weed. "This some good shit right here, son."

"That Tiger Bone ain't gonna have me skeetin' off on no ugly broads and that's fo'sho."

"Whatever…this Hydro is what's up."

"Word, it's that dro or what?"

"I got some at the crib, son," Show said. "Give me a sausage biscuit and I'll break your young ass some."

"Fuck that nigga! If that shit is like Viagra or something then I don't need that kinda help, dog. Just give me a good-looking broad wit' a nice ass and I could handle myself. Twist that that Dutch, Squeeze."

"Yeah, speaking of a nice bitch, I saw your physical this morning on her way to school," Show said. "I swear that her ass looks kinda fat. Its ready, son." No sooner than the words had escaped Show's lips, I was all over him, the 9mm in my hand.

"Aiight, you got jokes, right? Let's hear how we laugh when this gun's in your mouth, nigga! Fat mutha-fucka!" I said, grabbing my crotch.

"Y'all be easy," yelled Squeeze. "Show, here's the key to the ride. Here, catch this dog. Go to Mickey D's or wherever, bring me back some breakfast too, nigga. Go and stop fucking around like you gonna kill each other over breakfast from Burger King," Squeeze said and took out another sack of weed.

"Is that what I think it is?" I asked looking at the purple stuff.

Squeeze smiled and poured some out before yelling. "Yeah nigga, this from that white boy out there in New JeRoose," Squeeze said, then he began gently fondling the weed the way you would do to some new ass, Squeeze started running his mouth. "Oh yeah baby, this the bomb shit. This that Canada Dro shit," Squeeze said looking up, "And I know where we can get some more of this. Oh baby, it's so easy."

"Word?" I asked taking the plastic bag and inhaling the scent of the green smoky material. "It's sticky fo'sho," I managed to say as my mouth was salivating for more.

"That it is, bay-Pooh. That it is," Squeeze said. By the time Show and Promise had returned, Squeeze and me had smoked about two blunts a piece. I was getting open off the dro when the doorbell broke the spell.

"That's the doorbell," I said yelling above the loud surround-sound of his home theater system.

"Its probably them niggas. Get the door, Pooh."

I put the blunt down and walked to the door. Just before the entrance and off to the left was the kitchen with a security cam monitor. I peeked at the monitor just in case then I buzzed the door.

"Yeah it was them," I said and checked the name on the credit card stolen from the cutie.

"Promise wit' him?" Squeeze asked.

"Yeah, da nigga's coming up too," I replied once again becoming engrossed sifting though all the credit cards. Her name was on a W4 form. I asked again, "What the hell is a

W4?" I showed the form to Squeeze. He was older; he should know what it was. I waited too long for the answer. "Man gimme that..."

"Chill, I'm trying to see what the shit sez," he answered.

"If you don't know just say you don't know, nigga. You ain't gotta be embarrassed 'round me. We boys, dogs," I said.

"Yeah, nigga, this got something to do with slavery and I ain't going back to that," he said not fully comprehending the information on the form. Squeeze just didn't want to admit it.

"I hear you, dogs. Maybe Promise will know. You can't know everything," I said.

Squeeze threw the paper back at me before continuing. "That got something to do wit' some kinda tax bullshit or something like that," he said sounding frustrated. He put pressure on himself like that because Squeeze actually believed that despite not finishing any type of formal school training, he knew everything. No one could tell him nothing. I knew he had a lot to learn, we all did. I didn't take it that personal.

"Whassup, whassup," the glad hands started when Promise and Show walked through the door. Like real family members, we'd embrace first every time we saw each other. It was always that way.

As shorties on the block, we had developed our own handshake and embraced each other right to left. It was unlike what anyone else was doing. It made us belong, call it gang related or whatever, going through the ritualistic embraces meant all was forgiven. And besides making us feel like we belonged to something, no one else had it, it made us unique.

Through the years, no matter how large the booty got we kept things civil between the members. That was a lot due to how Show was. Big, black, and ugly, Show was like an enforcer. He was down to getting in a nigga's face at the drop of a dime.

They all walked into the apartment. Show was in the midst of stuffing a Mickey D's breakfast sandwich into his huge mouth, when he and then Promise walked in. They both carried food bags.

"Yo, does any of y'all niggas know what da fuck is a W4?" I asked and waited but all I got was chomping sounds accompanied by slurps of three hungry niggas feasting. "Ain't nobody trying to help me out?"

"That's some shit that America is using to destroy Saddam and them Al Qaeda niggas" Show said. "We need that shit, son."

"Whatever nigga," I responded. Everyone else chuckled.

"What y'all niggas watching?" Show asked, changing the subject.

"Nigga, can't you see the news is on the mutha-fuckin' telly, mo'fucka." Squeeze said then added, "Nigga, you best go get your eyes checked because you're blind. The TV is only 'bout seventy inches wide."

"Word, Show, you need to get you bifocals. I wouldn't want your blind ass putting a cap in the wrong ass."

"Nigga, please, all I'm saying is change the channel, nigga. You know the news ain't nothing but some bunch a bullshit anyway."

"Aiight. Here's da remote. You find something else," Squeeze said and handed something that looked like a small computer to Show. He pressed a couple of the knobs, familiar with it as if we were at the arcade and he was hogging the video game.

Finally the reverberation of G-Unit sounds penetrated the room, framing each corner with the picture of the happy gangster family. My question was now buried beneath the need to eat. We were like brothers, able to laugh at each other's faults while we enjoyed the spoils.

I remember attending school and hearing other classmates boast about their fathers, the cop, the janitor, the lawyer, the dentist. I even knew a few who had dads that were locked up in jail. I remember not knowing anything about having a father.

I was age four and one evening after coming home from school, I decided to ask my mother then I thought about it and changed my mind. I was afraid what the answer was gonna be. Maybe it was better not to know. It wasn't until six years later when I couldn't take it anymore that I finally gathered enough courage to venture there with my mother.

"Mommy, do I have a father?" I asked not realizing at the time that I was opening a whole can of worms.

"Don't be so stupid, Paul. Everyone has to have a mother and a father. That is how life is created, boy. No wonder your damn friends call you Pooh-Pooh," she answered with a smile.

"I know that and my friends don't call me Pooh-Pooh. Its just Pooh," I said and went off furious. "Why can't you just tell me that I don't have a dad instead of trying to be so smart," I said angrily, stomping my feet and demanding the truth.

I may have learned something that day but it wasn't what I wanted. I found out that yelling at my mother and getting her angry will cause her to throw that nice flower vase at my head. Especially after she had her drink and smokes. Whatever! I was out the room and never mentioned it again. It stayed on my mind and I calculated how I was gonna asked her sixteen more times but I never did. Maybe it was a lack of courage or maybe I just didn't care anymore.

Through the years, I just saw my mother as a woman who just couldn't keep men and maybe that was why my father never stayed. My mother had different men and each would last about two or three months in the relationship. She would start saying things then and you know a nigga be quick to leave.

My mother, she was a nagging woman who quickly grew on you. For that reason I can't say there was any real family unity but I had nothing but love for the family God had blessed me with. If there were any questions, they were my family in name but out here on the street, my real family was the niggas in this room and my two guns for protection.

Me and my sister, Lindsay, we had different fathers. Her father, Kenneth Roberts, lived with us for a minute. He was cool and all at first, buying me Jordan sneakers and fresh gear. Every Saturday, he would take us to the Fulton Mall and we'd really be cool. I was about ten years old and he was such a good man, I almost started calling him daddy.

Three months later, after he started living with us, my mother started nagging and everything just changed. In the six months of living with us, our mall trips went from every Saturday to once in a while 'till he moved out and we didn't see him ever again. When we'd asked about him like, "Hey mom, what's up with you and Kenny?" she would look at us with rolling her eyes and seething she'd reply:

"Kenny's dead."

You can't blame anyone for the way you live your life, my mother would always tell me this: "You got to get da fuck up out of here if you're not going to school or paying rent."

I had my clique. From day one, we were down for each other. I watched their greedy mugs put the finishing touch to breakfast.

"Yo, lets get into some big-dog biz. Uncle, get da fuck out of here! This is not for your ears."

His uncle would disappear and we'd be four smoking kids grown into men. We ran the streets when everyone was coming up and we respected each other so much that we're like a real family. Promise and Squeeze were like the older brothers and Big Show was all muscles, no brain. They all tried to protect me. I was like their baby brother and none of the bullies touched me.

These ghetto soldiers were my peeps and although I didn't want to see them leave, I wanted what was best for them. I knew Promise, he'd be a good dad, and Show and Promise would probably raise their babies. I could see them pushing strollers and wondering what type of toys to get.

I yearned for my dad but knew that I'd probably never see the bastard. Stepfathers were the closest I'd come to having any type of role models. The niggas from the hood were the real family. It was hard to, feeling like you could never hustle with them anymore. Everything must come to an end, and anything that's really, really sweet, hurts even more when its time to let it go.

I remember when my stepfather would go off to work everyday. My mom and little sister would hope that he would make it back home. I would hope he didn't. It was that shameless contradiction I wore like bling. I hated any man who tried to be my father even though I may have wanted them to stick around for my mother.

"Go to school," he would tell me when he'd try to play dad. I used to believe in him until my mom told me he did all he'd accomplished with no high school education. When I found out that he didn't even have a high school diploma, he couldn't tell me nada. He'd try and offer the excuse that in his time, blacks weren't allowed to go to school. I'd leave the apartment early pretending that I was going to school but then I wouldn't go.

The reason was the distraction of the streets and the paper that had to be chased. Being poor, you had a choice to either stay that way or fool yourself into thinking that working for someone else was gonna make you rich. We were down for that dollar bill and the right to be on we specialized in taking everything but mostly yours. If a nigga cut any deal in the hood, we'd be part of it. Whether it be selling drugs or guns, we wanted in. The pimps, they were targets too. Taking their money off their hoes, lifting that dough out their snatch that was my specialty. Yeah, we did everything to make the streets ours.

Even though I breathe gangster, it hadn't always been that way. I remember being a shorty and Ma'dukes worrying all the time that her men would never stay in her life. They'd be around for awhile but after a couple months she would start whining and wake up from having dreams about them leaving. Then just like that, they wouldn't be back.

I didn't tell her that the reason they never came back was because she was always bitching at them. I just tried to explain to her that men don't like when they home and their women constantly be jawing. Any real man will leave and make home somewhere else. Maybe I said it all wrong. She wasn't trying to hear me. I finally told her after I'd heard enough of her,

"Ma, you just bitch too much, man," I said as I sat at the dinner table. We had just finished eating dinner; fried chicken, corn, and rice. The television was tuned to my mother's favorite show, 'Sanford and Son' reruns. My younger sister, Lindsay, was helping with the dishes. I didn't see the need for me to help. Ma'dukes never saw it my way and jumped under my skin.

"What, you don't think you should be participating in the damn house chores?" she asked as I was busy playing my Game Boy. Instinctively, I ignored her. That's when shit hit the fan and she started really yelling.

"You lazy cocksucker, you never do anything around here but sleep. What you think? You got a staff of maids or sump'n?"

I tried to ignore her telling myself it was just Ma'dukes. I tried holding my head but she got louder and aggravated the fuck out of me.

"You're always fucking screaming! Why?" I asked.

She was surprised by my reaction but kept going anyhow. I had to put a stop to it once and for all. Now, I've always respected my mother, let that be understood, but when she started berating me in front of my younger sister, that was total disrespect and peace didn't exist no more.

"You're such a lazy bastard. You don't work and can't even hold down a damn job. You're good for nothing," she yelled.

"You fucking bitch," I said, seething. "You wanna know the fuck why you can't get a fucking man to stay with you?" I asked with the bravery of a fool. Her face registered fear and I pointed my finger menacingly at her as I continued, "That's because you're a fucking bitch, that's why." I realized then that I couldn't take it back.

That was the beginning of the end of me living in that apartment with my family. It happened during a major fight when everyone goes all out, and to the winner the spoils. But there were no winners here. The streets were the benefactor. Now, I knew I had to go and really hustle for a living.

My sister, Lindsay, stared wide-eyed at me. Maybe she was embarrassed by all of this but we both were becoming older. Lindsay was in the 10th grade and was aware of mommy's temper. Her irritability along with an innate bitchy attitude was all it took for explosions after explosions. Neither of us had the guts to tell her until now.

"Come on, stop this yelling and cursing the two of you," Lindsay said but neither of us heeded her request. That night, I left and slept at Squeeze's. My nigga looked out for the night.

"Yo, so why the fuck you and your old earth be going at it, son?" he asked as he passed the blunt.

"Squeeze, dead up, I be chilling, doing nothing, you feel me? That bitch she just old and tired, man."

I smoke and passed the night away. The next morning I saw my sister downstairs on her way to school. She told me about what had happened after I'd left home the day before.

"Pooh, Show called, and mommy wants to know where'd you spend the night? She was worried over you. You ain't call or nothing," Lindsay said. "Gimme a few bucks," she added as she was about to walk away. I pulled out a wad of bills and gave her two twenty-dollar bills. "Thanks." She kissed me and was off to school.

That was a good thing, it turned out that she liked school. I didn't. I walked slowly up the stairs and went into my Ma'dukes apartment and sat on the bed, still feeling the weed from last night. It wasn't too long after before sparks started to fly.

"You smell like weed, your eyes are brown, you're high," she said bringing the noise to the quiet high of my room. I just gave her that stare which read I don't care.

"You're a fucking loser," she continued. "Don't you see all your friends going to school? But you wanna play *Mr. Bad Man* and not go. Well, I'm not gonna be around for ever and..."

I never gave her the chance to finish. I'd heard enough. "Shut da fuck up, bitch!" I yelled.

"You need to get the fuck up outta my place, Pooh," she said spitting venom. "Get the fuck up 'fore I call the police and tell them you dealin' drugs. Don't think I don't know."

I don't know if I was just scared about my mother calling the cops or what. I left for good shortly after she threw me out. About a week later, my sister contacted me telling me mommy missed me and how much she was worried about me. She wanted to know when I was gonna be coming back.

"Over my dead body, never. I ain't never going back," I said.

"She wanted you to know that your room was there and you were always welcome." We'd sit in Burger King and talk and I always made sure to break them off from my hustle.

I loved Ma'dukes but she really got on my last nerves with her man problems and her useless griping. I was 17 years old, living on my own, and things weren't bad so I gave my sister five hundred dollars and kissed her goodbye. I figured as long as she had my number, we'd be cool. But I wanted away from Ma'dukes. That bitch was crazy, loca!

Now I never did much drugs. I was strictly a baller destined to be the next Jordan but I never fully recovered from a severe knee injury and that put a strain on the basketball career. Since I couldn't ball, school became a drag so I quit.

I first got started at fifteen grinding in front of the buildings. They made me a lookout. My job all day was to just hang out, steer clientele my mans and them way and let them know when jakes were near. Two fingers raised high and my peeps would get rid of their works and be out. We developed early warning system that would go off if police came around and we stayed off those street phones.

Whether they were plainclothes or uniforms, the police had that distinct look and smell. I could sniff them a mile away. No one got bagged on my shift. I did that for two months and that was the period of my apprenticeship on the streets of New York.

By the time I was eighteen, I had established a small ring; getting coke and selling it to the Dominicans. Then hitting them up for weed and selling it to the Jamaicans at two times above the cost. I'd hustle everything you gave me. Broads that I messed with, they knew what was up. I'd be quick to send one of them to distract a customer just in case the product wasn't too good. A nigga be too busy looking down the bitch dress to even notice a switch.

I'd have 'em roll blunts with a particular degree of hydro then slip him a pound or two of something else. Suckers never found out until it was too late then I would always promise to make it up. They wouldn't remember because I would send two more bad ass broads to deliver. You get the picture. The streets had made it that easy.

There were some rough times like when we hit them cats from Tompkins Houses and the following day, them niggas bagged me on my way from a diner. That was crazy. I'd just dropped a broad to the train station. I was sitting in the ride rolling something and listening to music. I got hungry so I decided to walk down to a diner on the corner.

The niggas were coming from the diner and one of them recognized me. They approached me like:

"Yo, ain't you one of them mutha-fuckas from yesterday who jacked us, dog!?"

"I don't know what da fuck y'all got going on but you better back down nigga. I ain't the one," I said.

And before I could reach for the iron, someone cold clocked me. I staggered to the middle of the street and felt a couple more blows to my head. Backing up, I slowly paced myself not wanting to trip but not wanting to turn and run. Afraid that them niggas may shoot me in the back. I felt the blood on my cheek. I gripped the nine milli.

"Aiight, y'all niggas want it?" I asked waving my weapon. I had to show 'em that I wasn't no punk. Niggas dove to the side as I let off a couple rounds. "Aiight, y'all don't want none of this," I said and ran when I saw five-o coming toward us.

I quickly located my car, jumped in and hit reverse. The BM flew down a one-way, barely avoiding three parked cars on the right side of the road. My gear was soaked with blood. I checked the mirror. It wasn't as bad as it looked, but I had a bloody lip and my face was fucked up. There were no cops following as I eased onto Atlantic and headed to

Squeeze. I got on the horn and tried to holler at Squeeze. No one picked up on that side. Where are them niggas when you need them, I wondered. I had to find them and warn my ghetto soldiers.

By the time I arrived at Squeeze's place, my face had swollen some and looked worse than it felt. I checked down in the basement after ringing his bell upstairs. Niggas were in the basement. Someone buzzed me inside and when I barged in; the whole shit broke loose. Everyone was kinda fucked up behind that.

"What da fuck! Niggas bum-rushed us. Get your combat gears we going to war. We got to go see 'bout 'em boys." Squeeze was ready to ride and that's the type of soldier you could count on. As I went to the bathroom to clean my face, I could see that worried frown on Promise's mug. He was for real getting softer. But at the same time I knew he was a real *live* nigga when he had to be. I just couldn't fully figure him out anymore.

We rode on them niggas and again the cops saved their asses. But not before shots lit up their blocks making the whole place hot like the fourth of July. In a few minutes, an army of swat was at our backs. We had to get the fuck up out with the quickness.

Later, the nigga, frontin' ass Promise, wanted to be let out by his ride. Squeeze pulled up along the X5. The nigga quickly jumped out like he was shook and bounced. I'm thinking we going back to the rest to strategize on these niggas but I guess that wasn't the plan. That wasn't what Promise had in mind.

"Yo, I'll holla at you later, my nigga."

"Aiight dogs," Promise said without even giving anyone so much as a dap. No love and he was out with the quickness. I rode the shotgun slumped in silence.

"Yo, the nigga Promise turning into mush," I said and meant every word. No one responded but I knew it had to be on everyone's mind here sitting in the truck. It was plain as day. Promise was walking away from all of us. I wasn't gonna be kissing his ass trying to be a sucker and all. If it was over, it was over. That's all there was to that.

"Yo Squeeze pull over here, let me grab a brew, nigga," I said.

Squeeze steered to the curb by the corner store and I hopped out. "Anybody want anything from the store?" I asked.

"Bring back a six pack," Show shouted. Squeeze just nodded is head.

I walked into the store feeling like Promise had in some way let me down. The old heads had told me to respect the set. Promise had disrespected-big time. I copped the beer and left the store.

The three of us sat in the SUV outside Squeeze rest steaming blunt after blunt and listening to Talib Kweli's song 'Just to Get By'. No one was really in a talkative mood. I guess there wasn't anything much left to be said. We were like lovers torn. The streets had blessed us as a set. But now we were slowly realizing that we were drifting apart. I drank my beer feeling pathetic with a bitter taste in my mouth. I didn't wanna welcome the stay of the feeling so I made a move.

"Y'all brothers be safe," I said after guzzling my last beer.

"What, you out? You gonna be aiight, young un?" I gave Show a hug and gave Squeeze a pound.

"You're leavin' for real nigga? Yo why don't you chill and watch the game or something?" Squeeze asked.

"Nah, I'm out dogs. I'm a go fuck wit' a broad. Be easy y'all," I said with my thoughts in a flurry and jumped out the SUV.

"Yeah lil' nig', we gon' see you in a minute, aiight?"

"Aiight," I said as I reached my car and turned on the ignition. The realization hit me hard. I didn't want to feel the coldness that comes with being alone so I put in a call to a flame in Queens. I was in need of some TLC. She answered eager just like I thought.

"I'm sayin' to myself 'who dis callin' me?' And I took a look at my caller-ID and I just knew it was your fine ass. What's popping, sugar?" She asked with tail wagging curiosity.

"What's good, Charisma? I need you baby. Had an ill accident, gotta lay low for a minute, you know how a brotha does."

"And you know your girl, Charisma's here for you my sweetheart. Come on over, I ain't got nothing' but time, baby. I'll make you some o' momma soup and if that doesn't work, you know momma'll give you sump'n else that'll soothe ya."

"Say no more, ma," I said and headed to the highway towards Queens. For about seven days, I chilled with her. True to her word; she revitalized me with that good stew her momma taught her to make. And, oh yeah, the soup was off the chain.

Early Saturday morning a couple of weeks later, I was home alone jotting down prose when the phone rang. No one besides fam had this number so it had to be one of my peeps. I remember the surge I got picking up the phone and hearing the voice. It was Squeeze telling me all about Promise and his new broad.

Then he got excited talking about buying this nightclub. The plan was that we'd meet up in da club to look things over. I decided to check the joint out later. I put the cell phone down and continued to write. Later, I went out on the courts but left the hustling early. I slid back to the crib to get ready for later. It had been awhile since I hung with them niggas. There was a kind of good feeling surrounding the phone call it was a chance for all of us to get back together. For the past couple weeks, everybody had fell back and just laid low.

Promise and Squeeze had us to chill for a minute all along, I didn't rock with that flow. I was daily grinding on the streets of Brooklyn. Now that summer was here and things were beginning to warm up, niggas wanted to be out and about making moves once again. At least that's what I thought.

The time would be right again for us to see each other. I'd go down see them later and have a few drinks. It was Friday night and everything was popping in NYC, no other place I'd want to see, because of the heat everyone was out on the streets tonight. The phone rang and this time it was my sister.

"Hi, Pooh what's popping?"

"What's good, Lindsay? How's my sis?"

"Fine, I'm doing fine. Mom says to tell you hello."

"Tell ma I sez hi." My response made me think I kinda missed the old earth. "What y'all up to, love?" I asked quickly changing the conversation from Ma'dukes. I've never received a message before from my mother through Lindsay.

I knew my sister be faking sometimes but I went along with it. I thought as I walked around coordinating my gear.

"Just chilling, chilling. It's dumb hot over on this side. How's it over there?" My sister asked. She was in a small talk way trying to say something but not saying it. She must want some money and my mother was staring at her or something like that. I'd stop by if I could.

"The same way it is over there steamy hot. Sis I gotta take a shower. I'll try and stop by. See ya later," I said trying to rush off the phone but she wouldn't let me.

"Pooh, Pooh, mommy said to tell you to be careful, alright? I'll speak to you again. Bye," Lindsay said and I could hear the dial tone as I stood looking at the telephone. Not stopping to think too much of it, I headed to the shower.

I knew that them niggas would be fly so I went into my closet and got fresh from head to toe in black. Versace shirt, Von Dutch jeans and Gucci kicks. Dressed to the nines, I left the crib at a little past eleven.

I was frosty with a blunt of hash mixed with that bomb-bomb-zee in my hand and the nine in my waist. I drove slowly in the shiny BM, keeping my eyes peeled for Jakes or Jackas watching me. Nothing was popping off on da block, just the same ol'; hustlers, runners and heads from the drug game I could see through my rear-view. Boops blew by as I drove slowly down the Ave., lights flashing aiming to stop the next man. I u-turn easy knowing I was dirty, holding heat and a blunt in my hand. No matter how much hush-money I'd offer that cop, that mo'fucka ain't taking it and I ain't going to nobody's jailhouse tonight.

I wouldn't miss that DT's head if that nigga came at me. I'd practiced shooting that head off in my dreams ever since I was baby boy. I'd see team of cops like gangs roaming the hood. They'd ride through the hood like they ain't want you to forget who really running shit.

It's funny how whenever I got dressed up I'd do a drive through the hood listening to Jay Z spit lyrically on a track with the great, Biggie Smalls.

Jigga. Bigga Nigga how you figga
Hey yo peep the style and the way the cop sweat us...

Jay ripped the track as I and my thoughts tried to keep up. I could see all the small changes in the hood and wondered why I didn't just get out. Dressed as I was I could get into a college or sump'n. I probably could find a nice respectable wifey. I mean maybe I could really do something with my life besides my present hustle, not be just another street gangster.

Hit you back split you ...
Fuck fist fight and lame scuffles...

I'd floss, just a lil' sump'n I'd do while thinking of what else could I get into. I could try running my own biz, maybe set-up some crack houses and make some real cheddar. Then flip that on some legit shit and make that money work instead of tricking it all on dumb broads and mad hoes. That would be a good look, I thought as the track play-on.

Most hated...
Ill fated while y'all pump Willie I run up in stunts silly
...scared so you sent your lil' mans to come kill me...

Lost in my thoughts, I rode 'till I was in front of my moms Brownsville housing. This wasn't planned. It had been sometime since I had been back here. I sat outside sucking on a blunt gone dead. Another ten minutes passed before I developed the courage to go inside. I went upstairs and knocked on the door. Lindsay and her bright smile answered the door.

"Oh Pooh! Mommy, it's Pooh. You're looking really fresh, Pooh. You go boy…" She screamed and hugged me hard.

"Who is it?" I could hear my mother's voice.

"Mommy, it's Pooh. It's Pooh," I said. Lindsay shouted as if Ma'dukes was deaf. I saw her coming from the bedroom. Then we all met in the living room. The place looked the same but it somehow felt smaller.

"Why did you come over tonight?" Ma'dukes asked. I scratched my head trying to think of the reason but none came, so I didn't answer. "You must've known it was my birthday. I told Lindsay not to say anything. She must've opened her big mouth." I could hear the distinct slur so I figured she'd been drinking. Then it was confirmed when I reached over and kissed her.

"I ain't told you anything, right Pooh?" Lindsay screamed from the bathroom. She came back to the living room and we all sat around. "You looking real fine big brother."

"I knew it was sump'n why I came by. I left my sketch pad and…"

"And your notebooks, right? Ma found them the other day and put 'em up for you."

"That's good. I'll get 'em before I go."

"You still writin' them rhymes and ah…"

"Mommy, you know that Pooh told you it was poetry, alright."

"Whatever..."

I could tell from all the chatter around me that my sister and mother missed me very much. Unfortunately I couldn't stay too long.

"Happy birthday, Ma," I said and peeled off ten crisp hundred dollar bills. She beamed when I put them in her hand and kissed her cheek. For all she'd been through, my mother didn't look old at all. The way she was dancing around the living room had me forgetting she just turned forty.

"Pump that volume up," she yelled happy as the sound of Ludacris came on the radio. "When I move you move..." my mother sang along with radio. It was time for me to go. I kissed her again and my sister walked me to the door. "See ya later, Pooh," my mother yelled.

"She's riding real high because you pass-through, Pooh."

"Why you ain't remind me that it was mommy's birthday?"

"Well, technically it's in a few minutes."

"Oh you mean it's tomorrow?"

"Yep, I was gonna call you again and tell you to bring her flowers and a gift. But since you're here, there's no need to."

"Nah, that's cool, Lindsay. Tomorrow I'll bring her some flowers and we'll do sump'n," I said.

"That'll be really good plus you showed up tonight. I mean nobody was expecting you to, Pooh," Lindsay said.

I kissed her cheek and shoved a few hundred dollar bills in her hand. I didn't want to make this an emotional trip. I made quick on the goodbyes, hit the stairs and was out.

The night was still warm so I dropped the top to the BM and hit the Belt Parkway on my way to the spot downtown. As soon as I pulled up, I could see all the mad cuties waiting on the line. I knew it was going down. They'd already taken a peek at the whip. The rest would be their story.

"Did you see his ride?" I overheard one broad ask another.

"Damn, did you see who's inside?"

There was a buzz on the line as I walked by. The blunt had me lit. I was ready to mingle. There were plenty of nice looking broads, well dressed in their high heels. I vowed to find me sump'n to curl up with through the morning. My mind floated as I walked through the crowd. I spotted them niggas standing off to the side.

"He's here, that nigga Pooh! Whassup baby-boy?" Squeezed almost knocked me over with his hug. His grip steadied me from falling. I was released and then fell into the embrace of Big Show. We hugged for a sec and then I began looking around for Promise.

"Yo, y'all looking sharp," I said. "Where da nigga Promise at?"

"You looking freshly dipped, my nig. Da nigga Promise sez he'll be here," Show said and gave me another dap and hug. A lot of good feelings were generated at that moment and I'm sure me seeing Promise would have made it even better. Although it had been only a couple of weeks, it seemed like months, whatever it had to be the longest period the four of us hadn't been around each other.

"I had a boy, nigga," Show yelled. He handed me the fattest blunt I'd ever seen. I stuck it in my pocket and gave him one more hug. We patted each other's head like we did at the park when we had swatted someone's lay-up attempt.

Show was feeling very good and I know his son would be great at sump'n. We both directed our states at Squeeze.

"Wha' happen wit' you, big Squeeze? Ain't your woman pregnant, she should...?"

"My woman, my baby, I don't know y'all. That bitch probably giving birth to an elephant, I swear. It's been like a year now. The bitch come to me the other day and sez the doctors may have to induce labor and all that bullshit. Got a nigga stressed, I'm telling you," Squeeze said and threw his hands up. He reached for a cigarette.

"You must be really stressing dog. Cigarettes? Whassup with that, dogs?

"Can't you tell? A nigga stressed, dog. I got to go down south. When I come back up, we back in bizness, aiight. I need a break from that bitch," Squeeze said. Show and I laughed.

"We waiting on Promise, that nigga called. Sez he was stuck on the Long Island Expressway. That was about a half hour ago."

"Word, Show?" Squeeze asked.

"Word," Show said.

"We ain't gotta wait out here, right? Wha' that nigga doing in Long Island? That nigga bought property out there or sump'n?" I asked jokingly.

"Yo, that nigga got this nice looking chick from out there."

"Say word?" I asked incredulously. It was news to me. "That nigga got a girl?"

"Been..." Show said then Squeeze cut him off.

"Yeah, that nigga's over his baby mom's death. That nigga got a school-teacher-bitch, from out on the island, son.

Where've you been? This shit been going on for a minute now," Squeeze said.

"Yeah, you forgot? I ain't seen y'all in minute."

"True," Show said mulling it.

"Well give me the 411, nigga. Does she have a fatty? Is she a cutey?"

"She a dime, son and, she's supposed to be bringing her home-girl."

"Oh hmm I got it. That's the reason you're standing out here, huh?"

"Yeah that nigga wants first dibs on the shortie, aiight," Show said jokingly. "I'm a roll up inside this mutha-fuckin jam wit' Pooh then dogs. I can't wait out here for Promise I don't wanna miss any of these sexy asses walking 'round here."

"Man, I ain't waiting on no first dibs. Y'all know me. Don't act like y'all don't know me." Squeeze shouted, arms flailing, popping his collar getting louder just like reverends do, and laying the gospel on real thick on the sinners prior to passing around the plate for the offering.

"Go on and preach," Show said.

"Pass the blunt," Squeeze said and solemnly sparked it. We strolled down the Ave. puffing the way we used to when we were shorties coming up. The temporary euphoria followed us. People all around were tolerant. No one uttered a word in difference, no one complained. No one called the cops. We laughed hard when we heard someone say, "That sure smells like some good weed."

We all turned around and saw an elderly white couple smiling behind us.

"Want some?" Squeezed asked.

"No thank you, young man. We had our share of pot in our days," the man said and they moved on.

Fully bent, we drifted back to the club. Our weeded eyes peeled looking for Promise in the midst of the downtown party crowd. That nigga was nowhere in sight.

"Yo, it's kinda late. I don't know 'bout Promise," Show yelled.

"Hit Promise on the two-way, Squeeze," I said.

"I already did."

"He told me he coming through so…"

"I'm saying, dogs. It's getting' late," I said looking at my wrist.

"Be easy, you might blind me, you're blinging too loud, player," Squeeze said. "I got a little sump'n, sump'n too now." He grabbed the heavy cross of a platinum pendant.

"Aiight, aiight. Who can fuck wit' this pinkie diamond ring?"

"Oh, goddamn! You see the ass on that bitch, dogs?"

"Yo, so we ready? Let's go in this piece, dogs," I said, still feeling jovial.

We were able to walk right in because Squeeze and Show knew the cat promoting the gig. This was gonna be our new venture, party promotion and club owners. I wasn't gonna let Promise's new attitude affect the way I felt. Promise and his new girl could stay out there on the Island. I didn't give a what. It was good to see Squeeze and Show, I was gonna party. There were still lines of broads waiting to get up in the club. We were escorted through to the front entrance. I swear that some female drooled as I went by her. She must have stared too long at my eyes.

Squeeze was talking to his homeboy. Show was up on some other fatty. It gave me time to check out the club. It could be something major. I looked around noticing the amount of nice broads in the place. I'd never guess that we could hold this down. Squeeze was working an angle on doing exactly that. It should be a good look for us.

"Are you seeing these nice asses, Pooh?" It was Squeeze walking up behind me. "We gotta wait to get up to the VIP," he said. "Where that nigga Show at?"

"I don't know. That nigga just took off with a big-butt-cutie."

"How's the place?" Squeeze asked. He was so hyped whirling his arms that he almost slapped the broad going by him. "I'm sorry Ma," he said graciously with that hood charm.

Honey dip showed her pearly whites. She was a petite Spanish broad with ample boobs. Nice fronts, not bad. Her friends were equally sexy looking broads.

"Yeah, this place is definitely jumping," I said admiring the broad with big boobs.

"If you're wondering if they're real? It's okay they real. You don't have to reach out to feel all you have to do is ask I'll show you." She smiled and flashed some thirty six D's then blew us a kiss before she started to walk away, ass shaking.

"Honey, what's your name?" Squeeze yelled after her.

"From the windows to the walls this place is krunked, dog," I said slapping Squeeze high five.

"Yeah! It's gonna be pumping some real dividends real soon, son. Those same chicks are gonna make it all happen, legit."

"You'll always be a playa, nigga."

"You know it, Pooh," Squeeze said. He was standing closer to me and by judging from the look he had on his face, I could tell that he wasn't just talking.

On the streets where a single lesson could cost you your life, it was a given that if someone had done something, they'd either tried it already or knew someone close who had.

It was hard to get a person from the street to change how they played the game. It took more than soap and showers to remove the stubborn grime from your mind.

"What's this I hear that new pussy got Promise thinking of settling down?"

"Nah, son, it ain't just a matter of that."

"Nah Squeeze, Promise know, we playas for life."

"Man, its time even I do something else, son. Just like Promise with his daughter, now I got my seed on the way..." Squeeze started but I cut him off.

"Yo, but I thought we were family. Blood's thicker than water, dogs. How could Promise just make a decision like that without talking to his peeps? It's like cutting off those who you close wit'."

"True but ain't none of us need anyone's permission. I'm a grown ass man with responsibilities. Promise is a grown ass nigga too. Everybody gotta look out for themselves." Show walked over and handed me his cell phone.

"Promise, nigga. He said he wanted to holla at you." Show said. I stared at the cellular like it had germs.

"Man, keep the phone. The music's too loud to hear anything. Is he coming through?"

"Nah," Show said. Squeeze grabbed the phone and walked away.

"Oh, that pussy must be real good for him to just stand up his peeps," I said.

"He sez it ain't just about no pussy, son," Show said.

"I told you, niggas, Promise done got too soft," I said as Squeeze walked back to us.

"Yo, that nigga said he had a little problem and he ain't think he gonna make it," Squeeze said.

"Promise knew he wasn't coming from the jump."

"That nigga said his daughter's sick and…"

"You know that he front'n. His seed might not even be ill. He just ain't wanna come." "Probably don't wanna even be 'round us…"

We stood hands in pockets looking at each other then Squeeze said, "I'm gonna holla at my man. He's up in VIP, aiight? He da one making this jump off a blast. We gonna talk about being silent partners to start. I'll be back."

"I saw that honey wit' da fatty from da building. I'm a go bag that," Show said and both started to walk away from me then stopped. "You taking the walk young un?" Show asked.

"Nah, I'm cool. Aiight, dogs. Go do y'all thing, thing," I said just as two broads walked purposely into me despite me trying to get out of their path. "I'm sorry Ma," I said apologetically. Honey dip caught all our eyes and for that moment everyone forgot what they were about to do.

"You too fine to be sorry," one said as they walked by. They were both good looking broads.

"That guy with the hazel eyes, he's fine," the other said loud enough for me to hear. I could recognize their game.

"They probably lesbians," Show mused. "They're dimes though. Strictly dimes in da building, kid." His broad smile came next. "They look hot. Go get you some o' that, Pooh. They hungry for you."

"They feelin' you, son," Squeeze said patting my shoulders. I didn't need the encouragement. I was already pushing up on the broads.

"Hey Ma, come here sweetie." They both walked to me. "Me and my man here, we wanna see them thongs, sweetness." I said. They both turned around like dancers and shimmied their jeans down just enough for us to feast our eyes. "Hmm looking good, good looking. I'm a come see you later Ma."

"We'll be right over there," they said and walked away. "He's so fine."

"I see you got some girls."

"Nah, I came here to see my peeps and..."

"Yeah, whatever man. But on da real, I'm going through this process of trying to set some shit up on the legal tip," Squeeze said.

"Word, I was just thinking of that same shizit, dogs. On da real," I said excitedly.

"Yeah man, you got to get legit. You know in da streets nothing lasts more than a minute, dogs."

What Squeeze had said stopped me in my tracks. "But we can keep our thing going in da streets, dogs, we..."

Show had walked away and now hurried back carrying drinks. He was excited.

"Yo, yo, her friend is the bomdiggy, dogs. She's too fine for a..." Show's voice trailed off when he saw the grimace on each of our faces. Show looked sharply at Squeeze then at me. His head snapped back and forth like he was at a ping pong match before he finally asked.

"What da fuck is up wit' y'all acting like bitches!? Come on niggas, this is a party y'all," he said and then turned directly to me. "Yo, there's a time and place for everything. Pooh, you aiight, lil' nig?"

I was disappointed by everything and I didn't answer him. We all felt a bit let-down but Show still wanted to party.

"Niggas acting up in da club, like they got beef wit' each other. If you got beef let me know 'cause I brought the burner," Show said.

"What you gonna do, Pooh?" Squeeze asked.

"'Cause Promise got a teacher from Long Island as his bitch, this nigga acting like I should be kissing his ass."

"Easy, young un," Show said, "don't disrespect."

"Pooh knows me better than that. If he's gonna dis…" Squeeze started but I cut him off.

"Man, chill. You know I ain't talking disrespectful but…"

"Yo, Pooh, you smoke some o' that oohwee tonight before you left the crib?" Show asked with a huge grin developing on his ugly mug.

"Why you always trying to be funny, huh?" I asked and stared at him.

"You need to calm da fuck down when you talkin' to your elders, nigga," Show said.

"Elders what? Elders this!" I said, grabbing my crotch.

"Man…don't let me…"

"What?"

"You got a little too much tension in you, baby bubba. I ain't too far from taking your ass out in the streets and beating you like you my son."

"Yeah? That's da deal, huh?"

"Yeah nigga, that's whassup. You just be wildin' out too fucking much, young un," Show said and took a couple steps toward me. I didn't flinch. If he wanted it he could come get it, I wasn't backing down.

"What? Why you always actin' up? You da youngest but you be wanting to bring all this tension wit' you," Squeeze said. "It's like you always gotta prove sump'n. Yo man, there is too much tension between us. We gotta chill."

"Yo, this nigga man, he always actin' like he gonna bring sump'n…"

I felt all the angst had reached boiling point. "I got sump'n for you," I said knowing that the nigga Show would be too big to back down.

"Baby boy, ain't nothing but air between you and me. We can take it to the streets right now, dogs," he said, taking a step forward. Squeeze rushed to stop him.

"Yo, y'all need to settle this beef outside, aiight. I invited y'all here to chill and have a good time..." Squeeze said.

"Word, dogs, lets chill man. This is a big move for us. We came to show nothing but l-o-v-e. Why y'all fighting? You da bad guy or sump'n?"

"Yeah, I'll be bad guy 'cause I want us to flourish. Go ahead and say it. I ain't going nowhere. These streets belong to me and I don't want to let it go. I'll be that bad guy," I said.

They all stared at me like I was infected with the virus. For a minute, they gave me a look of sympathy but then we just stared each other down. My anger boiled and I felt like killing sump'n but no guns were drawn. From the look in our faces, we all knew that we were at the crossroads of our relationship. Promise had found himself another love interest and it had destroyed what we had built.

Now it was him, his daughter and some teacher bitch he had recently bagged from Long Island. Squeeze, he wanted us to lay low and both he and Show stood by Promise. That left me on the outs.

We were in the club with the music ringing and should have been having a good time. But how do you have a good time when you know everything is over? I walked away.

"Y'all gonna act all funny with a nigga, huh? I don't need y'all. I don't need none of y'all," I said.

"Yo man, lets leave that young un alone. That nigga's got issues with his mother or sump'n. He'll be aiight in da morning," Show said.

"Let's go up to the VIP lounge and chill wit' honey and her friends," Squeeze said. "Hold it down, Pooh. We gonna holla at you later, aiight nig.?" I heard him shout but I didn't hear the whispers.

"That nigga's gonna get his ass kicked again for doin' dumbshit..."

All I knew is I was gonna do me for a minute. I didn't need to be 'round them niggas tonight.

The sound of R had most of the partygoers stepping. I flipped my collar searching to find the two Spanish chicks from earlier who had shown me their thongs. They had shown interest earlier, they should be ready to get up out of 'em now.

I paced the club like a bloodhound sniffing for them broads. Party people danced and pranced in time with the rhythm. Everywhere people were screaming while I tried to pick up the scent of my prey.

I saw the big boob broad. She winked and I waved but I wanted that pair of ass that was on my mind. I'd have to give *big boob* a rain check. The music played on and I kept walking. Among the hard-noses flexing in the club and the wallflowers, I spotted them drinking and dancing.

I waved at a waitress and told her to bring the chilliest bottle of Kristal. She told me that due to the high price, I'd have to be pay first. She smiled when I pulled out the knot.

"I'll be right back," she said still holding that smile.

"I'll be over there," I said pointing to where the girls were. The Kristal arrived before I did and then it was game time. They were dancing with each other as I approached. I joined right between them pretending to be dancing around but really feeling on both their asses, sizing them up.

They were both good looking. I wasn't fucking with nothing but dime-pieces. That's what them two were. Their caramel tone was set off by jet black hair. They threw their hands up wildly, playfully flirting along with me. These broads were already two drinks deep and jovial. Tits bounced and waistlines were grinding as the girls displayed the rest of their wares. The Kristal got them sprung. They were about to pop out their thongs. *They would get this dick*, I thought as I watched them wind their waistlines.

We guzzled drink after drink reveling in the moment. They were what a nigga needed, a distraction to the little problem I had with my niggas. I wanted to let my stress off, and two broads would be better than one. A few more drink s and we were exiting the club. I staggered a little from the alcohol but I was aiight.

With all the alcohol inside us I watched as the girls skipped to the ride and we piled in. One of the girls was in the back. I reached in the ashtray and lit the clip I had been smoking and then we took off.

"What's your name, playa?" The broad sitting next to me asked.

"They call me Pooh," I said puffing.

"You gonna pass the blunt or what, Pooh?"

"Sure, but don't you wanna roll up sump'n from scratch?" I asked reaching around. Her eyes widened when I pulled out the sack of dro.

We rode through the city easy, the broad in the front seat next to me concentrated on rolling up while the other burned a cigarette. They were both cooling. I pumped up the volume on Sleepy Brown in the ride, dropped the top, and we steamed as we glided down East River drive.

"Lets head over to my place," the broad in the backseat suggested.

"Oh yeah, she just got her new place over there near Flatbush," the broad in the front seat said. It didn't matter where; I was gonna be fucking sump'n tonight.

"Where in Flatbush?

"Take the BQE. I'll tell when we're there."

It was early in the am hours and the Beamer zinged through the streets. The wind blew cool air into the car. I raised the roof as the temperature cooled somewhat. The broads were both quiet as the weed and alcohol seeped into their systems. A few minutes later, we pulled up outside her Brownstone. She must have been sitting on some cheddar 'cause the place was dope.

I went inside and the place was still mostly unfurnished. There was a bed and a couple chairs. There were no curtains and the windows were so huge, one could see from inside out.

"Make yourself at home, Pooh," one of them called out to me.

I remember reclining on the bed and glancing, without caring, around the bedroom area. Besides the bed there was no furniture and that made it seem bigger. Nice place, I thought easing back on the empty bed. One of the broads joined me. She brought some coke in a glass vial. She spooned some in her nose and set some off in a pipe. These broads were wild. I watched her wiggle out of her jeans and slipped her thongs out the crack of her ass. I loosened my shirt buttons and flexed in my wife-beater.

"Those jeans were so tight. This is much better," she said walking away. "Do you want sump'n to drink?" she asked casually.

"Yeah," I answered with a smile. "Bring a bottle."

She smiled and walked out. Then the other walked in. She had the red thong and the other had a black one. It didn't matter, they were both gonna be getting this dick, I thought.

"Where did Ariana go? I thought she was in here with you," she said and then walked back out. I eased around just in time to see two men crashing through the window. I was surprised but instinctively reached for my nine millimeter. I spun and a let off three or four shots hitting one.

"Ugh…" I heard before he fell and the other one started firing back. I returned fire and knew that I had to get to my car.

The .22 was in the ride. I had to get to that. I didn't know how many there were but I knew someone was going to die and I didn't want it to be me. I flicked the light switch off and ran to the door. It did not go completely dark as expected. There was light shining straight through the uncovered windows from the lamp on the street corner.

I tripped over the body of one of the girls. Blood ran through her exposed breasts. She had been shot in the chest twice. One of the broads was shot down so I knew this couldn't have been a set up. I had to get up out of this place.

No time for my shirt. I didn't want to just run through the door firing with my wife beater. There had to be about six of them now. I was running out of rounds. I peeped out the front door and fired twice to see from what direction the shooting was coming. Streetlight was limited and it was hard to see.

Streets of New York

I heard the scream and gunshots blasted close to my head. I ducked and dove from the door. Bullets went crashing through the door. Someone had a good bead on me. I stayed low and started firing. I figured they had probably killed the other broad and was coming for me anyway.

All caution quickly left. I wasn't familiar with the lay of this crib but I knew the window was near and was the easiest way out. It would surprise them muthafuckas and then I would be able to get to the whip. I could see my car from where I was.

I waited a few seconds, then as I heard the patter of feet against the floor, I fired a couple a times and jumped out the window rolling. I felt a shard of glass ripping my flesh but I wasn't ready to die and started to run to car. As soon as I reached over to open the door, I saw the wires ripped apart from the inside out. The guts of my car were on the floor.

"Fuck these niggas!" I banged the steering wheel. The car was no good. The whole electronic system had been dug-up and left all over the seats. I heard more gunshots.

"He's outside. The nigga went though the window…"

"Get that muthafucka! Don't let that nigga get away."

Shots hurtled by me. I had to get the fuck up outta there. I ran and dialed my cell. *No service*. Only in Brooklyn. I knew I had to get the fuck out with the quickness and I ran hard. Too late to get a cab and too early to see any bus, I hit the hard top and ran in search of a dollar van. I waved but most of the drivers thought I was drunk or crazy and swerved to avoid me. I looked back and saw them muthafuckas' headlights coming after me. I had to keep moving. Just as I was about to try the cell again, they were on me like fiends on a car parked on the wrong side of town. These niggas were coming for revenge.

"Yeah, muthafucka what you gonna do now, nigga?"

There was nothing left to do but high tail it out of the hood and try to make it to my hood alive. I kept going. In the background, I heard an explosion. They either blew up my car or that broad's beautiful place. I couldn't stay find out.

I was running too hard and ducked as headlights blinded me. It was them niggas. Fuck, they had a car. I got up and ran to the busy side of the road trying to find the subway station.

****

I knew I had been shot when I ran into the station and now I could hear the ambulance siren. I could see paramedics trying desperately to keep my lifeline going. Sometimes it's your turn and you never know when it would be.

Lying here on the gurney in the Kings County Emergency Room, I wished there was a point where I could've stopped before reaching this point.

I couldn't second guess but it seemed like I could have stopped when we were all in the park, kids growing up and everyone was sitting around except us. I could've stopped then but I'd gotten too close to my fam, Squeeze, Promise and Show, to ever think of letting go of the brothers I'd desperately craved. I saw us in the park running, screaming, and stopping every time a gangster walked by.

"That's who I wanna be like."

"Yeah that nigga real cool."

"Out in da streetz, that nigga is da man..." We would argue and make up stories, never worrying about what happens when you die. Who hurts?

I saw them now, hands wringing and heads shaking. All their faces flushed from fighting their tears back. We were just some shorties who came up on the rough of *do or die* turf. If this was the end, no one should shed a tear for me. I'd made my own decisions. I lived this life gangsta as I wanna be. Everything, all my mistakes were up to me. There was no one left to blame, my niggas.

They looked sad and forlorn. Hugging each other again and again. Embracing like they never wanted to let go. Anyone could tell that we were truly family and they had come to represent for their fallen brother. There is strength in unity. Every ounce of feeling genuine, this was camaraderie like I wanted it to be.

Everything was perfect except the fact that my loyal brothers were unable to tell that I knew what was going down with them at the moment. I lay stretched out on this gurney of death dying with this scene in my head. The look in their faces confirmed the fact that I'd forever be remembered as a gangsta. It was a good thing to see the faces of my brothers just before my spirit exited.

My body was getting colder and colder, but I could still feel the warmth of their hearts as they drummed for me. Don't mourn me, *ride* for my memory. I could feel them but images were fading fast. I heard their voices loud and clear.

"We gonna get 'em! We gotta get them back for baby boy Pooh."

Those words would guarantee my infamy because now there was nothing but love left between me and my brothers. We were as grimy as the gutter that was the blood of our lifeline. It filled our hearts allowing us not only to dream big and think great thoughts but to execute our plans like a team tailor made for championships.

The streets had nourished us and provided us with a way to support our external family. But in accepting all that, you had to live and die with the contradiction that the streets don't love anyone. The people who stick around to the end, they do. As my physical presence broke down, I could hear the hearts speaking inside my niggas.

"Yeah, we gonna have to go at Nine and his crew. Them muthfuckas killed da young un," Show said with bravery and pride.

"Yeah, we've got to ride on Nine and rep for Pooh. Don't tell me you're gonna front, Promise. Dogs, we gotta let them niggas feel us!"

Squeeze exalted the others with his gat ready to explode at the wrong people.

Nine didn't kill me... It wasn't Nine and his crew, I wanted to yell. It hurt when I realized that no matter how much I screamed they couldn't hear me.

"Yeah let's ride for Pooh," I heard Promise say and I knew his heart wasn't really into the streets anymore. He should pull out while he still could. He just didn't want the others to think he was a coward. It's all good 'cause he had showed mad love by coming here to see me.

I wanted to join them hugging each other when I saw the clenched fists. So many things I wanted to say to my peeps. Tell them how they helped me out in this life. My time on earth was up. You don't choose the moment when you die, you just know it will be the wrong time.

The look of hope and determination pushed the sadness away from their mugs. They filed out the way we did when we were kids, leaving the classroom heading for the streets, each of us a crutch for the other. I was the youngest and they'd be out there by the school gate waiting to protect me from the bullies. There would be no more waiting. My brothers would be going on without me.

As the doctors poked around, my body got colder and colder. I saw their backs and for the moment, a speckle of sunlight came through as the door opened.

"It wasn't Nine," I wanted to say it but couldn't. My fate was dying knowing my crew was about to seek revenge on the wrong man.

With their gloves and the surgical masks peeled off, the men in white coats mumbled as they walked out of the emergency room.

"Gosh, those bullets cause too much bleeding!"

"Yeah, I guess he's reached the end of his ride, anyway."

"What a waste... It's time for my break."

"I guess it's my turn to notify the next of kin."

Sadness closed the window from which my spirit departed. My body wrapped tightly captured and frozen in this darkness. Maybe I tried but I died knowing I just couldn't shake that feeling...it's eternal. That could only mean one thing ... It must be **the end.**

****

*Coming Soon – <u>Streets of New York **Volume Two**</u>*

Find out what happened with Promise and his daughter Ashley. And read all of the new drama that unfolds on the Streets of New York with Show, Squeeze and the introduction of new characters...